CRITICAL PRAISE
for
THE GANGSTER PAPALARDO

"... The novel defies conventional methods of writing and follows no pattern. The narrative is not in chronological order. It moves back and forth in the past and the present. [The protagonist] draws heavily from literature in his narrative. Being an English teacher, he freely incorporates literary characters into his life such as the three witches from Shakespeare's *Macbeth*.

At times there is more sanity in the world of the insane than in the normal world. In its most unusual and interesting presentation of insanity, the novel *The Gangster Papalardo* only reinforces this idea."

--R.R. Bowker, *BookWire Review*

From a letter to the publisher:
"...Tell your customers, if [they] want to read something that is not great in length but great in depth of human emotions, read *The Gangster Papalardo*..."

--Marvin Adler, Educator and retired President of the M.I.T.A. teachers' union

THE GANGSTER PAPALARDO
A Tale of the Nixon Era

OTHER BOOKS BY FRANK SOLOMON
THE MANIFESTO of CAPITALISM, eds. 1-8

THE GANGSTER PAPALARDO
BY
FRANK SOLOMON

THE LIGHT BRIGADE PUBLISHING HOUSE:
HARRISON, NEW YORK

This is a work of fiction. Names, characters, places, and incidents are not to be construed as real. Any resemblance to actual events, locales, organizations or persons living or dead is entirely coincidental.

First created 1976 by Frank Solomon as unpublished manuscript under the title *The Revelations and Ravings of a Madman* and later as *Ravings. The Gangster Papalardo* is a revised and rewritten version of the 1976 novel.

Copyright © 1978 by Frank Solomon
Copyright © 1982 by Frank Solomon
Copyright © 2003 by Frank Solomon
Copyright © 2004 by Frank Solomon

1st ed. ISBN 0-9625163-4-1
2nd ed. ISBN 0-9625163-5-X
Library of Congress Control Number: 2003099160

The Light Brigade Publishing House
180 Halstead Avenue, Suite 3C
Harrison, New York 10528

"Welcome to Haiti." ---- Graham Greene, *The Comedians*

NOTE

Dr. Llemuel Moore, the noted Jungian psychoanalyst, who died March 23, 2001, left me in his will the privilege of reviewing several of his closed cases with the object in mind of allowing me to determine what features of these documents might be of interest to other psychiatrists and to the general public. I was given the exclusive right to publish in whole or in part what I considered of special note, with the provision of course that all actual names, places, etc. be fictionalized. This provision has been adhered to quite strictly for legal reasons, as well as the desire to protect the privacy of individuals.

As the reader peruses this authentic text created by one of Dr. Moore's most profoundly disturbed patients, he will notice sudden shifts in location, time, and tense which are indicative of the narrator's psychotic disorientation. Had this been the work of an author writing a work of fiction for publication, we would attribute these abrupt changes to stylistic flourishes meant to dramatize the very pathology I have indicated.

In keeping with Freud's *The Psychopathology of Everyday Life*, mentioned by the writer in the ensuing text, certain misspellings – as well as other authorial peccadilloes – have been retained for the reader's contemplation, as these errors may lend insight into the narrator's malady. To point out just one *faux pas* – from Chapter Eleven of the deluded man's notebook – it is probably not without significance that an apostrophe indicating the possessive case is missing after 'Sejanus' from the phrase "...evil Sejanus *buzz buzz buzz.*"

> Dr. Maxwell Weiner
> Dept. of Psychology
> Harvard Medical School
> June 2003

The Gangster Papalardo

Chapter One

Where does one begin? Does one begin with self-consciousness as the literary elf waves you on? Should the anxieties of critic Bloom function to keep you from love of entertaining the invisible audience and letting your dark sibyl and monkey pride seduce readers naturally their slow way along the unsure – even fabulous – convolutions of your mind? If I commence with childhood, it is surely the case everyone will go into spiral puking. Like *K*, I cannot espy through the shit bound and shifting haze that warps my sight what I am accused of. The corpse of my discarded mind floats before me now in the form of a naked woman. Coward that I am and tripe's embodiment, let me begin with her my sentimental journey.

Victoria was nothing but a mournful dog. So it was a rebuttal of both good sense and sensuality that I should have foolishly hit upon her like some mad horsefly on goat dung. The wild diddling spirit of honest Masoch must have touched my rabbinical

3
The Gangster Papalardo

soul. The whole episode should have been dust bin bound, not found its way into the Grant's Tomb of dire memory to bother there forever myself and anyone who should read this manuscript.

The book was hers, but I grabbed it accidentally. A teacher's guide to the poems of Edgar Lee Masters and several poems by E. A. Poe.

"I believe that volume to be a possession of mine," she mooed flirty and all.

"I'm terribly sorry," the words bland, as I searched my film bank mind for what some handsome Vegas or Hollywood hot shot might produce at this juncture. Even bovine women have cunts. To me heaven was what heaven has always been to most men – nooky moist and warm. May my shade roast in hell for pursuing the conversation.

"You were very good, I must say, at that last English department meeting," she commented. "I'm Victoria Spaulding, by the way." We shook hands, as I thought *Captain Spaulding's Wife*.

I responded, "Mike Kapmarczyk. I apologize, but I do not recall you. New at Jimmy H. Doolittle?"

"Yes. Just got here. ...," and so on with the usual drivel and primate blather for making signs of friendship or feeling each other out for a possible fucking.

4
The Gangster Papalardo

My attention is drawn at the moment away from such musings to the portentous slipper on linoleum noises that insinuate themselves into my reverie. The man in the yellow bathrobe begins to shuffle diagonally across my line of sight with steps like one of those metal toy soldiers that my son has; it is as though his legs were jointed only at the hip and not at the knee. His face is without expression, the eyes dull and sunken, the upper lip and nose thrust forward. As he passes within a foot of me, he tugs at the lobe of his right ear, which causes me intense agitation, but I cannot look away. I am fascinated. He continues to tug at his right ear lobe as he moves away toward the murals at the far end of the sitting room. Charges of nervous tension travel along my spinal cord from my coccyx to the base of my skull; finally I avert my eyes, which are beginning to tear. I have been reminded of one of Victoria's friends and am filled with panic.

At present I am in the Louis C. Furr pavilion of the psychiatric ward at Godspell Hospital in Manhattan. It is 1969. I am obsessed with the secret police, which do not exist, of course. Obsessions give meaning to our existence. Where would we be without compulsion?

Tresojos. Three Eyes in English or simply The Eye is what they are called, but only in the South Bronx. Other burroughs have other names. Something out of *The Double* and Kafka both. No one is sure if these creatures have any official

5
The Gangster Papalardo

status. They seem half in our work-a-day world and simultaneously to easily maintain their distance on some telepathic level where alien intelligence gathers. Shakespeare's term *alien intelligence*. Their erstwhile partners always their sorry victims eventually. What does Banquo say? "...to betray's in deepest consequence."

Why *Tresojos*? It was once explained to me by a newspaper vendor near the high school at which I taught. One *I* for impractical down the pike. A second *I* for immoral. And a third *I* for illegal.

We became friends, Victoria and Mike. Robert Ardrey, I believe, educed in *African Genesis* the core of man's divine nature could be reduced to the constant need for excitation. Half heartedly I attempted to get her knickers off. And the moo cow sanctioned my letch-as-Freud routine. It met her need to confess and be the center of attention. All things in one. Fuck me. Fuck me. Fuck me. Transform me. Now enter my mouth with your magic wand and foamy sea broth thick with seedlings, so I hoped. She brought me dreams, lovely love rings, propped wide portholes to her odd soul. "Listen," Victoria might begin. We would be huddled like two hares in a rabbit hutch, the empty English staff lounge. It was understood my lips were sealed. "I had this weird dream Sunday night. You were in it."

The Gangster Papalardo

"Continue," I encouraged, ratcheting up my most masterly imitation of Carl Jung endeavoring to unlock the vasty depths of some melancholy spirit.

"I hardly recall parts of it. A list of debts projected on the ceiling. ...Justin, my husband, my cousin – old lardass Nancy. Several other people. My whole immediate family, the Purple Gang of Red Hook, Dr. Mike may imagine." She laughs meaningfully. "We were all seated at this long table. My mother's sequine shawl cascading down over her pleated skirt. ...Like black hair glittering with dew drops."

"What does this lyrical shawl mean to you?"

"She would wear it in church. Father Thessalas provided every pew with shawls in case a woman forgot. Cover those tits. Sacredness I guess. Or chill. Wait. There's more," she says, holding up a hand. "The large red fish was savored by all the guests – the one in the gold platter in the center of the table I forgot to mention. Like Blake's demon." She pauses. I nod slightly, as though ponderously examining all this bullshit. Then Victoria continues. "Baron von Munchhausen's likeness, riding a woolly mammoth, graces the side wall, framed in ebony. It is signed Leonardo."

"Did you tell your psychiatrist about this dream?"

"No."

"Why not?"

"Just didn't. I don't know. Our little daily

The Gangster Papalardo

brain tryst takes his place. I don't need him anymore."

"Do you want to go on about this dream?"

"Why not?"

"What do the list of debts mean that ornament the ceiling?"

"A group of roof high obligations. The demeanor of my beautiful illusion is soiled by this mundane list," Victoria playfully suggests.

"How soiled?"

"The diners are various moral chains that bind me to Catholic garbage. The Church nurses my inhibitions."

"Sounds like something you discussed with Dr. Eagelman."

"That's right. But my relations with him are not what they used to be or should have been in the first place."

"Raise the dead," I urge.

"Yes," she asserts with what amounts to wanton enthusiasm. "It's so rich in steamy material. The royal road to the black pit of my unconscious."

"Plunge on Baroness."

"Why Baroness?"

"You forget the reckless noble on the mammoth gracing the side wall."

"What do you make of that?"

"A fabulous beast that no longer exists driven by the greatest fictional fabulist in all of literature. The mechanism of displacement is in operation. I suspect the woolly mammoth represents your extinct relationship with your husband, driven by the author of this wild tale embodied by your dream. Your destination is the consciousness of its true meaning by way of psychoanalysis. You indicated that I was in this eclectic montage, my sweet. Carry on."

"We were playing a guessing game. I don't remember exactly what was said, but *mon père* whispers something about Beaumont and Fletcher. I have not a clue what he meant. He knows nada about literature in real life. Then you appear out of the Munchhausen oil, à la some Old Testament prophet. You stand at the table in front of me. That's all I can bring back, except you point toward the front door in the hallway and insist that I leave."

"Interesting."

"O yeah. My husband tried to put your arm down and I woke up."

"When was the last celebration which tied you together as a family? A wrenching experience no doubt."

"Easter time."

"What does Easter celebrate?"

"The Resurrection."

"What famous meal does Leonardo's finest work portray?"

"The Last Supper."

"The Passion of Christ soon followed. When did you leave your husband?"

The Gangster Papalardo

"Right after Easter."

"His fourteen stations of the cross do not one wit grieve you, dear Baroness?"

"Why should it? When your in a lousy relationship, get out before it turns into a championship brawl that destroys you both."

"But he has been resurrected in your dream. Do you want to resurrect your relationship with Justin?"

"I think about it sometimes."

"Let's continue our analysis, shall we?"

"Full ahead."

"A game was in progress?"

"Some awful guessing game."

"You can recall only one answer. Beaumont and Fletcher? Right?"

"I wonder why?"

"Yes. Who were Beaumont and Fletcher?"

"Playwrights of the early seventeenth century."

"Then what must the responses have been?"

"The names of authors."

"So what must have been the hints?"

"The names of plays."

"What plays of Beaumont and Fletcher do you recall?"

"I know only one play by them. *The Knight of the Burning Pestle.*"

"What are the two meanings of the word 'night'?"

"The hours between sundown and dawn and a chivalrous hero."

"Psyche's horn of plenty for Freud and Jung. What happens at night?"

"Sleep."

"What else?"

"Sex."

"What does a pussy cat hope for at night?"

"A knight with a burning pestle," Victoria laughed.

"When did this dream occur?"

"Last Sunday night."

"I'm curious. What did you have for dinner?"

"Salmon. I burnt it."

"What kind of red fish was on the gold platter in your dream?"

"A salmon."

"Was this platitudinous fish in a more edible condition?"

"The dream guests devoured it."

"Not condemned to the disposal unit?"

"Funny thing. I helped my mother cook the Easter dinner. In reality I fucked up the fish course. Lucky an entire baked ham was there for the eating."

"You're a culinary genius. How did hubby Justin respond to the ruined *poisson*?"

"He was annoyed. In fact we didn't screw because my husband threw a tantrum over that lousy fish."

"So you went to sleep frustrated and in your dream the salmon of your last supper was not burnt. Wish fulfillment. If the salmon of your last supper – the meal at Easter with your spouse – had not been spoiled, you would have had a glorious night of sex with husband Justin and perhaps you now would not be seeking a divorce."

"You have withered my psychic boil to a mere pimple," she cooed with mild sarcasm.

Goaded to imply that my laudable analysis was deserving of a better fate than her contempt, I pressed on insistently.

"The pestle reminds you of what anatomical part?"

"A penis obviously."

"With which to crush medicinal ingredients in a bowl. Vessels of any kind represent female genitalia in Freud. Of what profession are the bowl and pestle a symbol?"

"An apothecary."

"With whom do pharmacists always work hand in hand?"

"Medicine men."

"What is hubby Justin's profession?"

"Physician. I understand."

"In your dream your loving husband was the knight with the burning pestle who would have given your vagina the sexual medicine it craved if the food had not been spoiled. In the familial Easter dinner that was spawned by your unconscious during sleep, the red phallus shaped fish – that large salmon – was dined upon with relish by an entire phalanx of your relatives, which suggests a dual desire to both fuck your husband and fuck your husband. You want a good lay from him and to castrate him for having damned you to a life of domesticity, which includes typical wifely chores such as cooking, which we have determined you're not very good at, your lack of skill resulting in a certain degree of marital discord."

"So what should I do?"

"Buy a cook book."

We chortled for several moments.

"Let me know at least what you were doing in the dream?"

"What do you make of it?"

"You would seem to be directing me to leave behind my entire past: husband, family, dinette set, traditions, unpaid bills, inhibitions, *et cetera*. I'm torn between liberty and giving Justin another chance, so I have him lowering your arm. Maybe I'm even attracted to you, well a little bit." She gazed at me warmly. Mission accomplished, I thought. Transference had taken place; id of victim aroused. Soon I would be able to get my dick in her mouth. Only I wasn't attracted to her in the physical sense. I had merely been fiddling around, staying in practice. A dangerous game to play.

The Gangster Papalardo

Chapter Two

Where do you begin to describe a day working at an inner city school? I had planned on speaking first about Shakespeare, whom I always taught, and by and by my students came to enjoy – well maybe a few from time to time, but it would appear too much like bragging. It seemed to me, finally, the right place should be the lotus eaters of which there were always five or six nodding gently as they snoozed in the back of my room. Each class had them periods one through eight, five days a week. The last spells were wonderfully free of addicts because the cafeteria was no longer in operation.

Far above the shitass knot of students attentively gathered near my desk, I rehearse the fruits of yesterday's cogent scholarship, before plunging into the mire and storm of *Macbeth*. "Many critics regard the Scottish play as Shakespeare's greatest. One element that all aflurry sets the pulses of these academic graybeards is the power of suggestion, perhaps more intense here than in any of the poet's other creations. The witching that provides us with the theme in Act I, 'Fair is foul and foul is fair,' hints that the causes and consequences of moral inversion are about to be staged. Why are the first words our thane utters, 'So foul and fair a day I have not seen'"?

One hand then another vibrate to my dulcet tones. Young and lovely Miss Rodriguez has set her heart on answering my initial probe. My teeth hurt when I look at her. She'll be the death of me. I would like to probe her depths and were I ten years younger, sober reflections might not be enough to keep me from doing so, hard though the wooing of a high school lass always will be. Terrible risks for her instructor, notwithstanding his experience and wily nature.

I expect Portia Rodriguez's answer to be above par, as I assume the responses of my other students will be also, since a list of today's pivotal questions at the last session were given them all. She is recognized.

"To emphasize the theme of the play," my love brightly responds.

"Good Portia. But our playwright could stress the tragic theme in a hundred ways. Why should he introduce his protagonist with 'So foul and fair,' etc.?"

"It's more powerful coming as *his* first words. The soul of Macbeth in three little words, 'foul and fair.'" Portia is brilliant. I am getting an

The Gangster Papalardo

erection. Thoughts of her pussy are making me salivate. A delightful tingling lightly trips along my spinal cord, far more thrilling than any poetry. I would sacrifice everyone in the Bronx just to be able to lick out her sugar plum pudding cunt for fifteen minutes.

"Why should Shakespeare echo what are the words of the witches in one scene in the mouth of his hero two scenes later, before Macbeth has met the three sisters? Mr. Brown."

Sean Brown is my best student. He makes sounds like a beached Orca when he has an answer.

"Perhaps The Bard intends his play to dramatize extra-sensory perception. Mental telepathy may be the real subject of this work – the cloak and dagger character whose shadow is all we ever see, like the silhouetted hand of a killer or the unspoken subject in the imperative 'Slay Duncan.'"
A profound interpretation.

Nurse Rose appears on my left. She smiles at me and begins speaking a moment before coming to rest. I cease writing, and know with a certainty, surpassing knowledge, that Dr. Rathbone desires the pleasure of my company.

"Medication, Mr. K," she says, handing me a cup. It is Thorazine, which makes you feel as though the business of life was all about gently floating in a huge jar of syrupy formaldehyde at the Smithsonian. A shelf to myself. A room of my own. I rise and begin to shuffle – indeed *shuffle* is the

The Gangster Papalardo

word – with tiny steps toward the seat with a cushion on the opposite side of the hall. When I finally arrive, another gentleman plops down beside me. It would seem he is about to confide in me. He leans forward and removes his blue chapeau which had adorned his bald but shapely head. He turns the hat like a rosary, slowly in his small hands.

"Mike," he commences. "This is not Victoria's fault." I do not make a sound. The man says nothing more, but poises nervously on the edge of his chair like a honey bee anxious to take flight. He makes gruff noises in his throat and some moments later takes off without a glance in my direction.

This whisper of disinformation creates ripples in my mind. They slowly expand. Victoria's name brings back ancient images. In the distant past who said that and why? Was the man in the blue chapeau *Tresojos*? Did they send him?

I have returned to my pad and pencil – again trying to describe for the patient reader a typical tense day at James Doolittle High School in the South Bronx. Mr. Shapiro and I are patrolling the first floor, and we decide to go down the street to Pete's Café for Cokes. The piercing shrieks from police cars greet our ears on the trip back. As we round the corner, three vehicles of the local gendarmes race in our direction up the street and veer to a stop at the building's front entrance. An EMS seconds later also brakes to a halt. As we enter

17
The Gangster Papalardo

the hallway from the lobby, I see cops taking away Pedro Montez in handcuffs. Something like this is not rare, but I happen to know the boy and he is in my view a good kid. So I go over to the attendance office where some people are milling tentatively about, and try to pick up some scuttlebutt.

"Tried to hijack Miss Pickle and the entire office to *Mejico*," Bill Silverstein banters. 'Miss Pickle' is our sobriquet for Gwendolyn Sheiskopf, the little Nazi who runs the place like official Gestapo headquarters.

"What happened?" I insist.

"He's telling the truth," Viv Pendoffski says.

"Almost knifed Gwendolyn. Chased her around the desk. Went after Flynn too. Nearly cut him. But Flynn was able to distract Pedro while Sheiskopf called the goon squad." These observations are offered by Norman DiCroesus who co-chairs bio.

Nick Flynn comes over. "I know this kid. It's not completely his fault. It's the system. We have some pupils working with us because the load's too big and they make mistakes. He kept on getting warnings about his cuts at home. Mama comes to school, makes a fuss. The kid denies ever cutting. Gwen checks each class carefully and sure enough the Mex is right. Mama does not speak American so good and gives him a verbal dressing down before our eyes in their very own *lingua franca*. But the cut reports continue home. We finally discover another Pedro Montez who was transferred by Livingston Street two months ago. Before I can call Mrs. Montez with the good news, she has missed killing Pedro by a hair because she doesn't believe his story. She raises some awesome welts on the kid's back and thighs. He gets a big carving knife and you know the rest."

"Shit. Unbelievable," I say.

"I'll say it's shit," Flynn seconds.

"I know the kid. He's in my first period class. He was always right on time, every day. Never absent. Today was the first time he was absent. Never late. What will happen to him?" I ask.

"They'll transfer him," Viv replies.

I pass Shapiro all this information as we take our last stroll around the first floor. When we come to the auditorium, Shapiro notes the hour and says he's got to piss.

"See you tomorrow, George," I reply as he walks away.

* * * * * * *

I sit down by myself in the dining room of the madhouse. Utensil noises bring to mind the famous line from Tennyson, but I am too far gone on these stinking drugs to accurately remember

19
The Gangster Papalardo

'windy Troy'. I have become one of the lotus eaters. And at the very thought of those dead souls in the assembly hall at Doolittle, I become even more depressed, too depressed to swallow a single morsel. We never used the vast room for any other purpose than to gather together the lotus eaters who were nodding from their shots. Some three hundred or so every day. Every day. What a whore is time. It seems thousands of years ago, *far on the ringing plains* in the olden days. ...

Two men seat themselves at my table. Uninvited. But they have a right, so I do not object.

"I'm Ben," says one man – a fat idiot – holding out his hand.

"Mike," I respond listlessly.

His friend says, "Jay. Jay Elphinston." I shake with him also.

"Mike," I repeat. "Mike Kapmarczyk."

"Why are you here?" Ben asks.

"Depression," I manage to respond.

"Depression?" queries Jay.

Ben leers at me and whispers *"Cannabis."* I am really startled. "What?" is all I can manage.

"Can you pass the salt?" Ben asks, looking at me with a quizzical expression, an edge of annoyance in his quiet voice.

"Cat got your tongue?" Jay asks.

"No. No," I nervously reply.

My God, I think. These are policemen sent by The Eye. *Tresojos.* Narks. The constabulary. But in the last year I consumed one stinking weed at a friend's house. Jesus. Maybe I heard wrong. Perhaps this louse did not say *cannabis*. Perhaps he only said "Can you pass the salt?" His tone did evince irritation. It could have been my reaction to his completely innocent request. He had merely wanted the condiment and I misheard. The feared aural hallucination. So I conclude that I should ask Ben why he is in the booby hatch – a sign of friendliness. When I turn toward him, I am shaken to see the man smoking a Benson and Hedges and blowing rings toward the ceiling. This simple performance makes me break out in a sweat because the act is moored to my aural hallucination regarding *cannabis*, which seems now not to have been a distortion at all, but a proper echo of what this gumshoe had carefully pronounced. Was I a madman or under surveillance? Just because I am paranoid does not mean three eyes is not after me. I am nauseous with fear. Involuntary responses have been triggered. Panic stricken, I rustle up the balls to excuse myself, and Jay says, "See you later," as I shuffle slowly toward the lavatory.

  I have just talked with Pedro's special education guidance counselor to see what can be done by the school to shelter him from the more harsh penalties of law, as his rage was hardly gratuitous. My steps have taken me to the fourth floor which is divided into an enormous lunchroom with one long, white corridor on either side. If one

The Gangster Papalardo

thinks about it at all, the entire floor is constructed like a crouching tiger. And this idea undoubtedly is brought to mind by the bedlam roar that engulfs the area. It is a miasmic stench of noise, prehistoric and awful. I enter this jungle through a door more sturdy than the thick portal that shut King Kong on his side of the wall. The crescendo rises as I pass toward the center of the beast where the kitchen is located. Is it likely the board of education ever inspected this repulsive sty and apery in full swing? No sane man would have let it continue in operation. Three dope dealers are wending their way, within my line of sight, from student to student. Heroin, cocaine, angel dust, reefer, all are on sale. It is a drug bazaar.

Past the kitchen, midway down the other wing of the hall, the school's drug 'czar' is talking to a uniformed cop. The 'czar' is 'Jumpin'' Joe Scoppetti, the boy's dean, who has sworn to get rid of the dealers in the school. Amen. As I glance in Scoppetti's direction, I see the police officer's head jerk forward abruptly with a chair careening across the back of his skull, flung by an impassioned scholar no doubt. At almost that precise moment, another lad smashes 'Jumpin'' Joe across the back of his noggin with a baseball bat. Joe falls in slow motion like some character in a Peckinpah classic. Another boy hits the vanquished dean with an industrial size garbage can as he is face down on the floor. Then the three clever lads race for the exit and are gone before the dust can settle. I am shaking. I notice a security guard kneel over the two bodies and leave them a second later at a clip to trail after the three shits, while speaking on his walky-talky. The students from the east side of the lunchroom have surged toward the west side, bunching up in rubber-necking and bobbing swirls around the two bodies. Some girls and boys are dancing on the tables and their ghetto blasters have been turned up. The air vibrates in a volcanic tumult that shakes the cafeteria floor. Miss Pat Gale stands outside the door of the literary magazine office, covering her mouth with both hands. Stretchers arrive. And three security guards are hard at work pushing back the crowd. I turn and leave.

After the last session of the day, I go downstairs to the English office to run off some mimeographed sheets for my evening school classes. Sid Ragouzza is seated at the communal desk, marking papers. Mrs. Gloria Pomerantz, the department chairperson, is barking on the telephone at some poor book merchant, from what I can tell. Sid asks, without looking up, "You hear what happened?"

"I was there," I say.

"Talk to me."

I describe what happened. "I know he was taken to the hospital. How is he?" I ask.

"'Jumpin' Joe is not dead, thank God. He's in stable, but critical condition at Montefiore. He'll be there a month or two probably. Fractured skull,

The Gangster Papalardo

broken collar bone. Very lucky. The cop is out already. Just knocked unconscious for awhile."

"Well that is good, as these things go," I say.

"Scoppetti is an idiot. A real knucklehead," Ragouzza remarks.

"Why?"

Ragouzza pauses as though contemplating whether he should divulge the fruits of mind shattering research to me.

"I hate to spread rumors," he begins. "Scoppetti signed on as dean with the specific promise that the school would be drug-free within a year. You recall?"

"Yep."

"He's sort of fixated on the idea. Right?"

"I don't talk with him that often," I respond.

"Did you recognize any of the assailants?"

"No."

"That's because they were intruders. People recruited for the purpose of giving notice to 'Jumpin'' Joe that his services were no longer required. A little memo from Don Carlo."

"You're kidding."

"Look," Ragouzza says, enumerating points on his fingers as he speaks. "We have circa one thousand hard core drug addicts here in this school out of maybe five thousand students on register. Add to that the twenty-five to thirty intruders we get buying or selling each day. Correct me if I'm wrong. Each kid spends in the vicinity of ten to twenty shekels a week on shit in our lunchroom. Perhaps the take is fifteen thousand a week. That adds up to lots of cash on a *per annum* basis. Maybe the mob can squeeze out half a million from a place like Doolittle. Maybe more. But no matter what you do, it can't be stopped. So avoid getting hurt, at least. That is why Scoppetti is an idiot."

At around five I go downstairs to get a bite to eat. As I descend from the second to the first floor, I see some Yahoo has taken a shit in the middle of the stairs. I nearly step in it and gag. Gingerly, I move around this defecation. When I reach the landing between floors, I shake my head and melodramatically mumble the famous words of Mr. Kurtz. *Why not dispense with archetypes,* I think. *Offal must be the **sine qua non** of existence.*

The Gangster Papalardo

Chapter Three

Rathbone – Dr. Isaac Rathbone – peers at me with little wolfish eyes. He looks like Van Gogh's portrait of himself. That red beard and battered, knowing face, raw and intensely handsome in some hideous way. He is waiting for me to say something. And I realize he cannot be trusted. Irate is how I might describe my mood. But remarkably cool despite frustration and anger. I will not blink. He has betrayed the trust I placed in him as a man dedicated to helping people, to saving minds from endless misery.

Poisoned. Our relationship has been poisoned by the fat smoker and Elphinston. Who were they? The Eye? Was it unreasonable to believe that this British bastard would allow these verminous dogs to invade his office and my privacy? He must be afraid that they could influence the immigration people. His green card might be revoked. That was what had been on Redbeard's mind. I would see this shithead's career ruined.

The Gangster Papalardo

Hotshot psychiatrist allows the constabulary to listen in and take notes as you do a dance of the seven veils. Next stop Sing Sing. Who does not have something to hide? Mad bitch. They will dig up something to cover her. Or they will concoct a tale with fabricated evidence. What to do?

"What has been happening?" Rathbone finally says in a low voice, stroking his beard.

"You know what's been happening." I hope to impale him with my steely gaze and manage to maintain a steady tone.

"Why don't you refresh my memory," Redbeard suggests. A lawyer's phrase – or a prosecutor's – *refresh my memory.*

"You are cooperating with the thought police."

"Can you explain your allegation?"

"You have allowed *Tresojos* to listen into our talks, you whore."

"Calm yourself," Redbeard utters, betraying considerable anxiety. "Give me some details."

"I take a seat in the dining room. Two men sit down at my table. Neither seems drugged. They both appear deliberate and even seem to eye me attentively, too much so. With a leer, one of them says to me the word *cannabis*. But then he asks 'Can you pass the salt?' a look of irritation on his fat, butt-like face. So I think I may have mistaken what he said – an aural hallucination. Then I turn back, meaning to be friendly, and I see him doing an imitation of a chimney, puffing smoke rings up and windward. I infer from this that maybe I had accurately heard *cannabis*. So I get up and leave."

"And from this you infer that certain authorities are auditing my sessions with you?"

"That's right."

"Perhaps we can discuss this. Do you think?"

"It does not mean I will hear the truth from you or even decent guidance."

"Let's take a chance. We have nothing to lose."

Not a new ploy for Redbeard. Imperceptibly, I shake my head and shrug.

"Let's review this scenario. Had you taken Thorazine just before this meal?"

"Half an hour or so. Barely."

"So you were pretty groggy?"

"I trust so."

"Were you or not?" insists Rathbone.

"Yes. I was fucked out of my mind. I guess I would not be aware of the true condition of two other nuts. Is that what you want me to believe?"

"I am concerned only that you recognize what might have happened. Isn't it possible the two men you imagine were the constabulary were as groggy and morose as you?"

"Maybe."

"One of them said either 'Pass the salt' or '*Cannabis.*' Right?"

The Gangster Papalardo

"Maybe one after the other, beginning with *'Cannabis'*. It is possible that only 'Can you pass the salt' was repeated. Without it being played back on some sort of recording device, I can't be sure. Of course, the fat pig blowing smoke rings would seem to confirm my original suspicion." I pause with some faint hope of redeeming my sanity.

"Even if this 'fat pig,' as you say, did enunciate the word *cannabis*, it does not mean you are under investigation." Like a grotesque bird of prey in some Jungian *Alice in Wonderland* story, Redbeard rivets me with his condor eyes. "You see how confused your interpretation is? Furthermore, your history does not include a drug factor. So let us ask what in your background could have triggered this paranoid muddle? This mood swing?"

"I don't know."

"But you do know. You have discussed this with me on several occasions. What did you tell me you had to endure from your father over a period of three years, from the age of four through the age of six?"

"I don't know," I mumble, struggling to escape the brass cage of words he was fashioning.

"Your father will win this battle if you do not come to grips with what you told me. Repeat what you said about your screwed up relationship with him."

I gaze numbly at a picture behind Rathbone's head. The combination of the drugs they

The Gangster Papalardo

have been feeding me and my own fervent desire to believe all my problems are merely psychological induces me finally to obey him. "He used to torture me as a child. He would command I enter his room, and while drumming his fingers on the arms of his *chaise longue* where he reclined like some fucking magistrate, this piece of sadistic troll shit would accuse me of something I could not grasp at that age – four, five or six. He would force me to apologize. Dozens of times over three years. Then he went to a psychiatrist, Dr. Cama, at my mother's insistence. She threatened to leave him if he didn't get help, if my inferences are correct. Of course, there was also a slightly different sort of torture developed for the sake of variety and sheer fun no doubt. The Goody That Torments I call this game. He would dangle a piece of delicious candy in front of me and yank it away suddenly again and again until I became hysterical. I never got the great prize. ...Then there...". I cease my roll call of abuses when Redbeard holds up his hand to halt the recital and says, "You see yourself how a chance encounter with anyone at all tending to remind you of authority will trigger a paranoid response in your mind? You respond to things in an immature way, pathologically introjecting events which have nothing to do with you, twisting each of them into a court of false accusations, accusations such as your father made against you as a child. You become overwhelmed with paranoid guilt. The innocent patient, your ugly fat man, becomes a culprit. The other man becomes a co-conspirator no doubt, and I am nominated for the Chair of Grand Inquisitor." Rathbone peers at me with the ferocious curiosity of a vulture bent over a dying wildebeest.

The Gangster Papalardo

Chapter Four

Unlike most males, it is not strictly true that the one thing I contemplate is screwing. I struggle to keep my mind on various other aspects of life, such as eating, reading, and the art of pedagogy – at least those parts touching on E. A. Poe in the *curriculum* or Shakespeare or the English Romantic Movement. A whore – however – a good whore, a pretty whore, is more likely to capture my adoration than the loveliest verse of Shelley or Keats. And the Turtle Bay Cove of such a delightful nymph is what I now seek as my much-battered chariot braces to defy the noon traffic on Second Avenue.

I make a left to go east toward the river, as thoughts polymorphous perverse germinate in my brain. I salivate with lust at the memory of those mythic breasts, whose perfect protuberant aureoles haunt my dreams and now cause a pant intermittently to escape from my throat. I am not aware at first that my own physiology could be creating this distinctive overture to the fucking and delicious sucking anticipated in the lofty heights of brick impatiently being approached. The imago of a racing Great Dane slides into view beside me and I panic. How can I exit this ancient Thunderbird with that canine slobbering outside? He will no doubt fasten his teeth on my awesomely swollen tool and chew it off. After the car has come to a halt, I recognize the mastiff delusion my ventriloquized panting had magically summoned into consciousness. Biblical. My *amor* had fashioned the beast of guilt that would punish this infidelity. Don't hobnob with whores and avoid castration.

Quietly the elevator rises toward the twenty-first floor where Briseis awaits her Achilles. At least that is what the whore says is her first name. In matters of love, it's Greek to me, and I want it to remain so. But the panting does haunt my imagination. Those strange emissions of passion – strange only because of them issuing from outside the car it seemed. Would a passenger have thought they came from the street? If not, then I had disowned my need out of guilt. Even had I thrown noises like Edgar Bergen, it was an attempt to avoid having to face a battle with myself. Shame has made me a cur.

"Who is it?" she finally asks to my frantic pressure on her bell.

"Mike. Mike Flynn," I rant. Of course I had never told her my true last name. She opens the door a sliver, not fooling with the chain until she is

The Gangster Papalardo

sure it is the client who called.

"Bri, it's me. Mike," I say.

"O yes Mike," she mews, undoing the chain.

I grab her, push my lips to her mouth and begin to purr involuntarily as I stick my tongue between her teeth. Our tongues meet as I clutch Bri's perfect little ass with both claws. She places her hand on my cock and lets go.

"You're hard as a rock. Wait." She twists away and paces a few steps into the apartment.

"I don't want to ruin my clothes," I hear Bri impart as she disappears into another room. "Make yourself at home. How've you been?"

"Fine," I answer, moving into the living room. "Should I take my clothes off?"

"If you like," she yells.

I strip down to my underpants.

Wearing nothing now but green panties, Bri undulates before me and smiles with a smile that knows what it is doing. I fixate on her wonderful breasts, my breath shortening. In one hand she holds a lit joint and bends toward me.

"Smoke?" she asks.

"Suck my cock."

"First smoke. I want to talk."

So I put the reefer in my face and draw profoundly.

"Yesterday I had a queer experience." I weigh her words as she drags on the mary jane. We have this deal. I play Freud, absorb her pain for a while, and she gives me free sex. She begins again to speak. "I was walking Seagram. You know. My poodle. She's inside." Bri motions with her head. I nod and blow a ring.

"We were two blocks over, strolling west. A little man comes up to me and pets Seagram. You know at first I thought he was a customer. He begins to tell me about my father. Says he comes from Delphi, Greece near where my father lived before emigrating. Then this dwarf – he was no more than four foot eight or so, standing tip toe – pushes his mouth toward my ear and says sotto voce, 'All whores are forgiven in heaven.' I go to smack him, son-of-a-bitch. Even though I am a professional, you don't say such things. The little bastard slides away. Next thing you know I can't locate him, as though he disappears in thin air. So I go my way and forget about it. But last night I have this dream." She pauses and gives a sigh, twisting her hair back from her face. I peer sleepily at Bri, steady as a head of beer in a tranquil mug.

"I am walking in Atlantic City, on the beach, and there are these colorful green and white umbrellas that you might see at Orchard or Coney. I hear a circling gull call, but it never appears. I turn my head and look up, but cannot catch a glimpse of the thing. I am wearing what a guy like you dies to see your little naughty nymphs in, a gauzy see-through night gown with nothing on underneath. It keeps blowing open in the wind, exposing

The Gangster Papalardo

everything. My teats, my cunt, the whole business. Then there is this very large, black bird hovering in front of me with immense leathery wings, like a prehistoric flying dinosaur they have in the Museum of Natural History. I forget the name. I once saw a reconstruction. Pterodabill something I think. Maybe. The other people are all dressed in these old fashioned nineteen twenties bathing suits made of wool you see in photos. Men are wearing striped tops and bottoms. Not one of them so much as glances at me in the dream. Not a hard-on in sight. Then that schmo, the dwarf I told you about, comes like a shot out of nowhere toward me, kicking up sand. He is carrying an ice cream cone and his fly is unbuttoned. His cock is hanging out, but it looks more like a walking stick than a prick. He says, 'Your big penis, Princess Caroline, has been marking time at the gypsy's.' An old gypsy used to tell our fortunes in the neighborhood when I was a kid. And he holds up three Tarot cards, one of which I get a good look at. But it's one I don't recognize from the traditional pack. It is a Lady hanging upside down with no eyes and a dog's face. The face of Seagram – a poodle's mug. It has inscribed in fancy gold letters across the top, 'You must be bold to go to Delphi. Follow me.' I reach for the card and the little man runs off. I race after him down the beach, calling, 'Wait! My fortune has not been told.' Without a trace, the dwarf vanishes, just as the motherfucker did in real life. And I wake up. What do you make of it?"

"What you make of the dream is what counts," I say, my stomach knotted in desire. It takes an hour and a half to analyze the piss she has told me and before we can get to fellatio.

"O Bri honey, you have stolen my heart," I gasp, as she pulls down my shorts.

First, in heavenly puffs up and down my engorged member her gentle mouth pursues a litany of "God...O God...Please" that issues like a dying prayer from my partly open lips. Then lightly her tongue, in tiny flicks and kisses, pirouettes and ripples around and around the head of my aroused shaft. As she slowly draws the head of my manhood into her maw so moist and warm, she holds my balls and daintily slips a finger up my ass. I paint the air with moans and sighs at her exquisite touch, as she lowers her head and coquettishly looks up at me with the wide, green, innocent eyes of a pre-teen caught stealing from her mother's purse.

"Do you like it?" She stops and pouts.

"My God, yes. I do. Don't stop. My God don't stop." I can hardly breathe.

With an adorable smile, to my seething cock, Bri bends again. And now she slows and quickens the magical pace that owes a step to time, nestling softly and softly troubling my ecstatic boys. I nearly pass out as she tightens her savory lips and twining tongue in a final coda on my resonating flute.

The Gangster Papalardo

Eruptions of scum burst from my staff in fast, thick pants like the crater of the world in explosion, and these mighty gusts – at once immense and joyful – seem to go on forever. With elegance, every hot effusion Bri greedily gulps like sweet mother's milk. Then she kisses my lips.

"Thank you. O thank you. I love you Bri," I manage to say, almost in tears.

If God exists at all, it is in the impassioned exchange of bodily fluids between consenting adults. Or so one might imagine at such times.

The Gangster Papalardo

Chapter Five

Again it is time for our medication. A weary line of patients form a queue that stretches down the hall akin some surreal South American snake dipping its head in the nurses' station for a sleepy sip of nepenthe. If I had not made bed my home, I would be more like McMurphy in *One Flew Over the Cuckoo's Nest* I kid myself. Breaking up the place. Kicking ass. The girl in front of me utters a sigh of dreadful resignation, responding it would seem to my forlorn dream. I think of Jung. The collective unconscious. I love synchronicity. So spontaneous. So Shakespearian.

The man in the yellow bathrobe is standing behind me. He tries to push past on my left side. But I won't let him. I stand like Stonewall Jackson at Manassas. My ruin would follow in the wake of his successful incursion since I know he would tug on his right ear lobe. And this cannot be allowed. It is a row of grave significance. A battle of position. But now my attention is drawn to the two pale and

The Gangster Papalardo

hefty looking chicks posted straight from a production of *Ancient Porn Stars on Display*. I think they may be speaking about me. Miss Shit Mound and Miss Rat Squeak. I can read their lips, a skill at which I have become rather adept since the beasts have taken to harassing me.

"My goodness. Isn't it sad. You can hear the feasts of grotesque thought being gobbled by his detestable soul. That's why they harass him you know. He projects his mind. Doesn't give it a rest. Interferes with just about every person on earth. They hope to kill him one of these days. Sooner the better, I say."

"Good riddance," responds Rat Squeak.

"He's a son-of-a-bitch," Shit Mound emphasizes. "We pay taxes to have this asshole teach our kids. Shhh! He's listening to us. Really, it's so sad. We're too far ahead in the line. The stupid piece of shit thinks he can read lips."

Am I really able to read the lips of these cunts? And if so, to what degree am I accurate? These are the notions that come to mind after the reptiles maul you.

I shuffle into the little sitting room where they have a phonograph and records. I put on one of those forty-fives. Jack Jones's *Never Lovers, Always Friends*. It does seem fitting. Maybe too fitting. A single fact could be a mere coincidence or one could deem it an instance of Jungian synchronicity. Could someone have planted it beside the machine? Was *Tresojos* prone to such subtle tricks? I guess all kinds of shit was up their alley. Kafka. Indeed, even, one might say to stretch a point, Orwellian.

During the fifteenth rendering of Jack Jones's song, a fellow patient I call Old Man Mountain ambles into the room backwards. Mountain is about seven feet tall, unshod. But his hobnailed boots increase the impression of his awesome perpendicular advantage and suggest that reason and great caution ought to transcend other approaches to this troubled soul and spectacular primate. He seats himself gingerly and brushes back his shoulder length salt and pepper locks. A beard trim is needed by this aging giant since that appendage, in falling rings, now ends at his navel.

"My boy," he begins familiarly, although we have barely nodded 'hello' in the past. "Man is famished for justice, and justice is not dead so long as we base it on science, bare boned fact, and an objective assessment of the damage done the long term *bona fide* interests of Caesar. Are you innocent?" He gazes at me with eyes the size of plums.

"What is my sin?"

Mountain pulls gently at his beard. "We have not decided yet. Maybe we'll let you determine that yourself. Your fate is up to you."

"It does not seem I am very much in control of anything," I venture.

The Gangster Papalardo

"We have no intention of deciding your destiny and perhaps not even your crime."

"Continue."

"What is justice, Michael?"

"Proportion."

"Can you expand on that?"

"Proportion concerning a man's relationship with others, particularly apropos his actions and connections to the ship of state."

"Well said. I doubt if I could have stated it better. Are you a lawyer?" Mountain probes.

"No. A paltry school teacher. The good Mr. Chips." It troubles me that I indulge this loon by answering his questions.

"How did such a concept sprout from this monstrous tub of swirling shit?" he asks, his eyes hooded now by monumental hands poised just over his brows and above the bridge of his nose.

"Did it evolve from the dynamics of group survival?" I query nervously, not wishing to incur the wrath of someone seven feet tall who might have gotten another notion of justice from his life experience.

"Imagine a jungle," Mountain directs in a John Huston baritone, dramatically crooking one immense yellow finger. "Bee hive huts in the Cainozoic, surrounded by an ironwood stockade. One tribe trying to survive with other savage tribes on every side set to invade at the slightest hint of weakness. To deter such aggression, the square mile hunting and breeding ground must be guarded constantly and its hunters must hunt with skill enough to feed a hundred males and females – the infant and the elderly – each day of the year. Drought costs them dear because the fish, fowl, game, edible berries and potable water disappear. They must gorge and hoard. Finally, the tribe buries its dead in mass graves, returning to dust all its lusty band of men and maids whose collective wits were not enough to discover the techniques of the smokehouse. He rues the day that gulps down Sunday's mead while dismissing thoughts of Monday's thirst. Thus respect is born for foresight, imagination, and intelligence. The group that does neglect these qualities ceases to exist. Shun such changeless states of mind." Old Man Mountain pauses now with theatric grace. Tenderly he strokes his beard. Then he begins again to speak. "A particularly cunning hunter appears on the scene and instinctively realizes that he has a very safe and easy area in which to cheat. As the mainstay of his tribe, he must decide when, what, where, and how to bring down game. First he has to slay enough meat to fill the common belly of his clan. But because his superior hunting skill, within the tiny circle of this savage horde, knows no peer, he alone finds ample time each day before dusk to catch and roast a rabbit or two for his private gluttony. Then he wends his way home and according to custom, in front of an elder, saws off the sovereign slices that

The Gangster Papalardo

are the stalker's proper wage. Stomachs are full and no one so far is aware the hunter has been double-dipping. Eventually he gets caught of course. A court is convened consisting of the king, his chamberlain, and one or two other worthy advisors. They are confronted with a very profound legal matter. Had their paramount hunter used all his time between dawn and dusk to bring down game for the entire tribe, they could sing his praises now because their level of caloric intake and nourishment would have increased they conclude – making a rough estimate – by one hundred percent. Should they execute their economic mainstay for treason? They could have protected their land and women more adequately had they been better fed. More wives and parents would have been saved from an early death. However, to remain free of famine and the increased risk of invasion and extinction at the hands of the Ubangis next door, they can't behead him as ancient law demands. And they can't cut off an arm or leg or pour hot lead in his ears without destroying his talent as a hunter. If they humiliate his Spirit too severely, he might offer his services to another savage group, with results predictably sadder for themselves than if they had killed him. So the king and his advisors decide to decree Apollo had committed some small offense, in the future have a 'guide' and two other hunters track with their boyo on daily excursions, and pare down his stipend to less than heroic portions. Has justice been done, Michael?"

"No."

"Well said. It is good to remember that it is always easier to haul an innocent man before an officer of the court than to try a guilty pillar of the status quo for capital crimes he actually perpetrated. Till we meet again, my friend, adieu." Mountain elevates himself from the chair and walks backwards out of the room. The Jack Jones's torch song is still playing.

A hunting story? A fishing expedition? Was his anecdote intended to mean anything or was his parable just the ravings of a deranged mind? The Eye? Testing my reactions? *Cannabis. Cannabis.* It is these speculations that drive me to seek the services of a lawyer.

The Gangster Papalardo

Notebook Entry, September 23, 1969.
I have had an odd dream, if you will forgive the redundancy. But it was neither some bucolic phantom nor a nightmare. It was something in-between the two.

I was struggling to get through a door which was too small for my height or girth. A head appears sporting a brand new lid. It is the stovepipe kind. At first sight I know the hat to be recently purchased because a label is sticking out that reads one and three sevenths. A worried looking face with a very long snout eyes me from the other side of the door. "Why do I yield to that suggestion poor fool?" the mouth says.

Then I am sitting at a picnic table with my children, playing *Clue*. My son places the gun in a patio. He giggles and gives me a wink. "It's Colonel Orwell in the Plaza with Larvae," he says. Then I wake up.

The Gangster Papalardo

Chapter Six

She had said that there had been strange people. Queer people. Odd people. Dreadful people. In the psychiatric institute where April had been placed. After the rape. The rape perpetrated by that medieval monster. That Sicilian ape scum, the gangster Papalardo. Now I remember the distinctive little man in the blue chapeau. He had tried to convince me that the Sicilian woman, Victoria, had nothing to do with my being here. As that man tried to convince April that Papalardo had not raped her. Strange people. Odd people.

April Evesin and I had been lovers some six years before. Eventually, our lovemaking had become a sorcerer's delight of magical moments and feverish days. But things other than ecstasy were abed and more than the telling will bare.

We had met at a dance in the early sixties catered for the less than smooth professional by the Plaza, which fared pretty well at five dollars a head. Bars had not yet started becoming those bee-hives

The Gangster Papalardo

of neurotic mating that led them finally to transcend in garish magnitude all the ploys mothering nature in the past had created to bring male sperm to female zygotes.* Instant fucking with total strangers and one night stands would soon replace the beau's torch a crooner's voice once toasted.

That encounter in a charming ballroom of the Plaza Hotel became the still point of the turning earth for me, and my doom it would seem. Of all the beautiful fillies I had blundered with, April Evesin I imagined would be the most exquisite. No hymns or songs or trilling cantos touched by the genius of Keats could have crossed the barrier between her loveliness and his words. Nor could a mountain of erotic lays etched with the steamy finesse of Petrarch, Byron, Spencer, and Shelley in every phrase have caught those faery queen eyes whose pacific green luster reflected light like eerie lamps on the pearly bottom of a tropical and perfect ocean. Her coiffured locks were as black and richly flecked with tiny fires as sheen and night could make them. Features that would have improved the

---

*The word should be *gametes*, rather than *zygotes*. I have reviewed every test and interview re. the case history of the writer of this manuscript. Thus, I can confidently affirm that he would have known the difference between the two. So this error must be categorized as a Freudian *slip of the pen*. And it has considerable significance appearing as it does in a chapter concerning his great love. – M. W.

work of Leonardo graced the good lady's face under soft white skin. I needed to ravish her more than I wanted to live.

She allowed me to lick out her fragrant cunt on the second date and rendered me an angelic blow job that can't be had for money. Thank God for Freud and transference.

As flip as I may sound dear reader with that last line, April had real problems, and not the kind that could be cured by pithy musings or a new hat from Lord and Taylor. We had sex dozens of times every way imaginable, save cock in vagina, during that fine September. It took me a tub of butter and thirty days to unlock the gates of heaven so that I could slip my weiner inside. The reasons why I had to wait so long form the buttresses of another part of April's account.

About a year after we met at that seminal dance at the Plaza, she related the entire story to me. I sat down at her instructions, preparatory to having a pattern of dreadful details traced on my mind. We had been having miraculous sex and her tensions had considerably diminished. We were thinking of taking our relationship to a new level of endurance, so the narration of her powerful tale of woe was prefaced by soft kisses and the warning, "At this point I have to tell you something, even though my mother told me not to repeat the story." She paused nervously. "Something happened to me three years ago, ... before we started dating." April stopped

The Gangster Papalardo

speaking again and wet her lips. "You remember how gentle you had to be when we first made love?" I nodded, stroking her arm. "Why was I so tense do you think?"

"You're young, inexperienced, inhibited, shy, fearful. It's normal. I thought it was charming."

"Do you remember that you were trying for about a month to get my legs apart?"

"Yes. They were like iron. Locked shut."

"A little more than you might find in the average young woman, don't you think?"

"It never occurred to me. You were a virgin."

"That is not strictly true. I lost my virginity to a rapist. I had been raped."

I looked into those mysterious green eyes and swore to myself I would not crack up. But so deeply was I in love with her that every word she said began to move the landscape of my restive soul like the tremors of an impending earthquake on some quiet and distant atoll.

"You know Madeleine Trafficante, my friend?"

"Of course." I had met Madeleine Trafficante twice.

"One day about three years ago, I was on the way to her house. I got off the bus in Sheepshead Bay. Her house is about two blocks from the bus stop. You recall her father is some sort of capo in the Mafia? I told you."

"Yes. I recall you telling me," I said.

"As I approach her place, I see this new Lincoln Continental beside the house, against the curb, idling. The driver calls to me and I recognize him. A casual acquaintance I knew from high school. Pasquale Papalardo. I go over and inquire what's he doing, blah, blah, blah. Small talk. He asks me to get in the car, blaisé and all, you know. I laugh and say 'no' of course, knowing all too well what he has in mind. He had opened the car door so we could talk. Then he grabs me by the wrist and pulls me into the car. He was so strong, I couldn't even move. I couldn't scream because he pushed his disgusting, ugly face against my face and forced his tongue down my throat. I resisted with all my might. He ripped my panties off. I couldn't do a thing. I had been wearing a mini-skirt. It was over in a minute. It was dreadfully painful. There was blood all over the place. Then he let me go and I started screaming and crying." She began to weep now and put her face against my arm. I soothed her and kissed her head. She began again to speak.

"I got out of the car and ran up the stairs to Madeleine's house and banged on the door and rang the bell. I was hysterical. I heard the animal drive away. Madeleine opened the door and I babbled out this whole thing. I was pretty incoherent and Madeleine could easily see what had happened from my state and the condition of my clothes. Madeleine's mother and Mr. Trafficante came in

The Gangster Papalardo

and listened to me. Mrs. Trafficante and Madeleine looked pretty shook up and tried to calm me down. Mr. Trafficante listened to what I said and then disappeared inside." April wiped away her tears.

"Do you believe me?" she asked.

"Yes," I said. "Of course I believe you. Why would you make up such a tale? Of course it's true."

"I think Mr. Trafficante phoned my father and told him if he called the cops, they would kill me. Papalardo was close to their family I found out. A wannabe Mafioso. One of their budding leg breakers. There's more." She was dabbing her eyes now with a handkerchief. "Two days after I was raped, I was lying on the couch with a splitting headache. I had the television on and suddenly began screaming and weeping. I had a nervous breakdown. They put me in an institution. There was a man there who was trying to convince me that Papalardo had not raped me. But I knew he had. There were other weird people there. It was dreadful. Some of these people were frightening, terribly frightening. Then I came up pregnant. They tried to convince me that I had sex with someone in the madhouse. But that is not true. I know it had to do with Papalardo, with the rape. I had nothing to do with anyone in that place. In any case, the Catholic Church allowed me to get an abortion. The asylum was connected to the church. But I could only have the abortion on condition that I did not bring it to a court of law, that I did not press charges. We had to sign all kinds of papers. That is the whole story. Do you believe me?"

"Of course. Of course it's the truth."

"I had to tell you."

I held her and we kissed gently.

"Do you care?" she asked.

"Of course I care. My God, how could I not care? My angel. My baby." We embraced again and I kissed her hands.

"I mean do you care that I wasn't a virgin?"

"April, if you think that I am stupid enough to care about something like that, you do not know me. I care that you were raped, that you were injured. But I think women should have all the sexual adventures they desire. And with this birth control pill, they will. I love adventurous women. But what happened to you was done by brute force. That is not an adventure. It's a nightmare. Don't you think I'm intelligent enough to know that?"

"It was the Mafia."

"What do you mean?"

"It was a conspiracy. It was a premeditated rape."

"How is that possible?"

"I am sure of it. You don't know these people."

"Look. I believe what you say is true about the rape, the hospital and all, but why in God's name would the Mafia be involved? They're just

The Gangster Papalardo

businessmen."

"To gain dominance. To show me and the Jewish community that they are the boss. They're always trying to do that."

"To show that they're the boss?"

"That's right. You don't know these people. Do you know Papalardo offered to marry me? But I wanted nothing to do with that ugly, revolting piece of shit."

"Of course not. But just because this animal was Italian does not mean the Mafia was involved. That's like saying when you have a car accident that General Motors conspired against you."

"He is Sicilian."

"So because he's Sicilian, the Mafia must be involved?"

"I'm sure it's true."

"Look April. You're an extremely beautiful girl. And you are very sensuous. When you walk down the street, every cock stands at attention. If we weren't lovers, I would rape you myself."

"But you wouldn't use force. You simply mean you would be aggressive."

"Of course."

"And you would stop if a girl wanted you to stop."

"Yes. Of course."

"That's not rape. He used brute force. It was horrifying, terribly painful."

"I believe you. But I'm trying to show how a

wild animal like Papalardo could have raped you entirely of his own volition, having nothing to do with the Mafia."

"I know it was the Mafia," April insisted.

The Gangster Papalardo

Notebook Entry. September 25, 1969.

I am writing in my journal like Winston Smith. Again.

It is through intimations that we process life. The witches in *Macbeth* take suggestion, a product of nature, and use it to pervert the regular progression of historical events. What they do is unnatural, you would imagine – otherwise Shakespeare being Shakespeare would not present them as hermaphroditic creatures of the night – as any act can be thought unnatural which deliberately mimes one of nature's secrets, to radically influence for very bad purposes the fey Scot's behavior. *Why do I yield to that suggestion/ Whose horrid image doth unfix my hair?* And die for a red herring, a false clue, that borrows its vehicle from an old play? If my memory serves, *whose murder yet is but fantastical*, a development rhymed with the theme so adroitly, *fair's foul and foul is fair.* Telepathically communicated. *So foul and fair a day I have not seen* are the first words as they come on stage in scene three. Macbeth's first words. They *are* his very first words. Which hints they're using thought transference to snare their victim. A form of suggestion. If you realize its unnatural, that it is coming from offstage in effect, you find yourself in danger of being systematically harassed into insanity and murdered. If you have adequately and effectively psychoanalyzed yourself, as I have done, the idea appears instantly of some sort of carefully orchestrated conspiracy. It becomes a terrible distortion. A simulation of the spirit of paranoia, a replica of those very effects we find in a nightmare as Freud makes clear in *The Interpretation of Dreams*. *The Interpretation of Dreams*. A devil's handbook for The Eye. And a very short time later they let you know it *is* The Eye. The bastards *confirm* your paranoia. You are having a normal reaction to the card some opponent has cunningly played to mislead you in the bridge game of life. Panic ensues. You regress to hysteria. They will kill you for defense of the Reich. The status quo that is history for special interests will bring about your doom. And what if they don't fling in your face the false or true intimation of *Tresojos*? Well then, you simply have a nervous breakdown. One more day of *Catch 22*.

The Gangster Papalardo

Chapter Seven

Ben the fat man has taken a seat beside me on the radiator. He manages to startle me out of a trance into which I had been gradually phased by the shit prescribed to lull us. The fat man begins to speak, and he sounds like a scythe slicing through cotton candy.

"Cincinnati won the ball game 'cause Duff Reynolds can hit triples and gets on his bike galloping *cannabis* jail time – can a' peas – left field wall to Nigger Jim floats off the raft up your butt this April appease Papalardo on his speed boat so he doesn't cut off your balls in the night sky during a time I don't trust doctors nor dentists so fuck 'em all, but heroes sight unseen buck the system if a dumb whore grabs your cock confess says the law driven by dollars and wouldn't fool the kids if I had a wife..."

I get off the radiator in alarm and scuttle away, away from his frightening monologue, his psychotic and evil stream of conscious incitement.

The Gangster Papalardo

I return to my room in psychological agony. I wrap the pillow around my head, and with both hands tightly hold it in place as I sprawl face down on the low bed. The bed is actually no higher than a mattress with tiny stump legs. This is to prevent patients from shying themselves onto the floor from perilous heights that would do them injury. I cannot block out the shrieks of the lunatic next door even with the downy pillow pressed against my ears. As soon as I relieve the pressure on my auricular appendages, the screams orbit around my head like wasps having a tizzy fit.

I assume the fetal position in an attempt to escape the present horrors that assault my senses. The din somewhat abates after an hour, so I am able to contemplate the very bad situation in which I find myself. The fat man means prison I surmise. He is a functionary of The Eye. Vividly I imagine the homosexual attacks that will turn me into a woman when my sadistic jailors vote to throw my ass in with the menagerie of two thousand psychopathic killers and rapists who make up the general population. The guards will be taking bets on how many minutes I last before death mercifully closes my eyes. In response to these thoughts, I feel my dick shrivel to a tiny ball and reach down my pants to see if in fact anything is left of my fragile manhood.

That Catholic bastard. But how do I know Ben's Catholic? He may be Protestant. Or even a

The Gangster Papalardo

Jew. But by all measures, the sadistic pile of rotting elephant shit must have been brought up religiously. Only religious institutions, with their brutally wrought effects on the human mind and their sinister epistemologies, could bring into existence such a group of gratuitously evil scum. Torturing bastards. I am dead. Christians. They will bray like hideous donkeys at my funeral, glad to be rid of the kike and his species of subvocal talking, those barely audible whispers that haunt their minds and subvert their childish ideas about God. What an awful catastrophe their primitive and sick dish of medieval puke has brought mankind. What could be more natural in a madhouse than delusions of persecution? What could be more consonant with why and how psychotic minds work than aural hallucinations? Who will believe a lunatic? Why am I here after all? Loosely defined, I fall like some nutty Punchinello north by northwest of that reliable bedroom hamlet of pat answers and evenly mown lawns. Sensitize the bastard. Show him who's boss. The familiar made terrifying. Let him advertise elsewhere his twisted nature and imbecile mind.

At that moment there is a knock on the door.

"Mr. K," the voice of Nurse Rose calls softly, as softly the door glides open of its own accord it would seem. A long nose, an eye, half a mouth and part of a chin ominously appear. Relics of a Dali illustration for a Breton manuscript.

"The doctor will see you now," the woman

intones cheerily. Right on time. I'll tear the lips off that fraud. That tweedy scum bag. That fatuous, evil, little limey from the backstreets of London or Surrey or wherever the fuck he was spawned. Once I enter his office, he will be dead before I leave it again. Bring me a really good chainsaw my heart shrieks.

"Coming nursey," I say, careful to give the perfect imitation of a healing patient in order to hide my consummate and awful rage.

Rathbone is seated at his desk. He does not look up. He assumes the posture of The Disinterested Man. The objective scientist. Not a co-conspirator at all. How could he be? The gentle and humble psychoanalyst. His feet are resting on his desk. He smokes a pipe and is in the midst of lighting it. I approach and pound my fist on the ink pad.

"I have been tortured. Tortured. You phony son-of-a-bitch."

Now he looks up. "If you do not get control of yourself Michael, I will stitch your mouth closed with sedatives so strong, you won't be able to talk to anyone for a month. Sit down."

This whole thing is wrong I think. He glares at me. This is no fun you can bet. I have misjudged everything. They can do to me what they did to Hemingway. Shock treatment. Foul play. A wreath on my coffin stating how my futile reliance on psychiatry led to suicide. Lobotomized. This fuck could have me lobotomized. I stumble back – into the chair. McMurphy's fate I ruminate. My brain could be sliced in two.

"What happened?" Rathbone freezes me with his most angry gaze.

"That fat pig was at me again. He ripped my head off."

"What do you mean? Be precise."

"That scum bag comes over to me and ties my brain in knots."

"How?"

"Stream of consciousness rigmarole. Nonsense. Idiocy. But he knew things about me no stranger would know. He interjected pieces of information. Little hints. Little clues."

"What clues?"

"About April Evesin. Other things."

"Are you certain you didn't imagine these hints?"

"He knew things about me he shouldn't have known."

"I will speak to him about it."

"Oh. So you concede something has been going on."

"I concede that another patient has probably been bothering you. And that is all. These things go on all the time in an institution like this. Patients are here because they are profoundly disturbed."

"It is conspiracy."

"You are overreacting. Let's talk about your

father."

"These techniques were used to kill the president."

"What do you mean?"

"They induced Oswald to murder Kennedy."

"Who are you talking about?"

"People. People acting in concert like the three witches in *Macbeth. Tresojos.*"

"What has that got to do with you?"

"It changed the course of history."

"Again. What has that got to do with you in this present situation?"

"If the murder of Kennedy had been investigated properly at the time, instead of being covered up, this would not have taken place."

"Your disturbance is the result of the Warren Commission you would lead me to believe?" Rathbone is now insouciantly lighting his pipe again.

"You are mocking me."

"No. I would just like you to explain the connection."

"People can hear me think."

"You must learn to relax."

"I stick out like a sore thumb."

"Do you think this effect is related to your experience as a child?"

"My father you mean?"

"Yes."

"Of course. It is the result of abuse, of

trauma. The Jewish Adolf Hitler."

Rathbone nods his head and looks at me with thoughtful and compassionate eyes. "Which of you is the real Führer?"

"I am to be sure. He was merely Fyodor Karamazov, although that is probably a bit too flattering for the real Dr. Kapmarczyk." Tentatively I am allowing myself to be lulled.

"And if he is Fyodor, what does that make you?"

"Smerdyakov?"

"You tell me."

"Well I wish to kill the dwarfish emotional development he has inflicted on me. So I guess that makes me Smerdyakov. On the other hand, both Dimitri and Ivan wanted to kill him, and since his terrible effect on me is still abundantly clear, I have not executed the old man. Therefore, I am a synthesis of Ivan, Dimitri, and Smerdyakov. It is Alyosha I do not resemble at all."

"Does the very process of attempting to purge his effect on you make you feel guilty?"

"Yes. I suppose it does."

My anger has been assuaged by Redbeard's acceptance of my assertion that Ben the Pig had been harassing me. So I find myself falling into the more relaxed mode of a patient conversing normally with his psychiatrist.

"You feel that purging yourself of this masochistic negative identity with your father is a breach of Mosaic Law perhaps, as in 'honor your father and mother'?"

"Rooted in evolution," I say in a low voice. Now I *wish* to cooperate with Rathbone because the very action of sliding into the commonplace suggests the wrath I experienced existed only to throw me beyond my subjective torments. It had been a makeshift construct. I do not really need a lawyer. I have not had idiots assault my mind with their snot-nose tricks. No one demonstrated any of *Tresojos*' frightening ploys that I might be stabbed to death for simply knowing.

"How?"

"The primitive necessity of defending territory in order to reproduce effectively, so that the tribe can survive. Really nasty males must be produced so that they can viciously murder all the members of a competing tribe if need be. Leave no one alive to seek revenge at some future time, except an infant or two below the age of three, for women who had not been able to have children and want a baby. Fathers must be ogres. Only the naturally ogrish could produce potential mass murderers who would obsessively identify with the tribe, its culture and needs so that all the outlanders would be looked upon as dead meat. In undoing the twisted nature of my identity, the perverse relationship I had with my father, I am simultaneously destroying this primitive desire to defend the tribal territory and its symbols. I am in

The Gangster Papalardo

effect voiding the very means of doing so, the terrible primitive pride and violence that might compel me to attack another person for a slur against Jews perhaps."

"Maybe it will lead to a more sophisticated way of defending Jews?"

"Maybe."

"Do you want to talk about your father? His teaching methods which you mentioned once before?"

"He decided I was stupid at an early age. Would not give me a chance. Wanted an excuse to bully me and take out his disturbances on his son. I remember once he brought home a jar from the hospital with two tonsils inside, preserved in some formaldehyde. Tonsils he had removed that very day. He held the jar up and began to explain to me in medical language far too sophisticated for an eight year old what the contents of the jar was all about. When I looked at it, although I felt no disgust, I feigned some revulsion at the tonsils by wrinkling up my nose and making a noise of loathing in my throat. I meant to be a little humorous. But he deliberately took this as an excuse to snatch the jar away and say 'With that attitude, you can't become a doctor. Too stupid.'"

"How did you react to that?"

"Crushed. How would you expect? And confused."

When I am released from Redbeard's court, I

lethargically shamble – as though caught in a tangle of leg manacles – toward the very sitting room where Old Man Mountain and I discussed the clash between necessity and the dispensing of justice. Five ladies are seated in chairs and on a couch. They are all in various stages of tasteful undress. Pajamas, nightgowns, robes. Debauchery is not their primary concern, however, even though my imagination flies to Prufrock and Degas. They would blithely spurn my crude advances. I doubt I could rise to the pathetic overtures of even the loveliest of these damsels. But then again, in their drugged state, advantage might be taken. Who knows what could transpire? If my performance were an outrage, what stunned and listless gal could scan such stuff? I am getting an erection. I sit myself down beside the youngest and most pretty of these women. She is knitting a scarf it appears.

"I guess that is for your husband," I say. A hiss greets my preliminary advance. It is followed by a longer and more pronounced expression in the snake idiom. It startles me. I feel it bore between my eyes. At that very moment, the distinct prattle of birds invades my hearing. From the corner of my eye, I glimpse the movement of an old hag's lips. The fowl parlance *does* come from the effort of those fleshy grubs I am horrified to realize. My head snaps back and away as though it were being wrenched from my neck by powerful claws, and I faint.

The Gangster Papalardo

When I awaken, it is beneath lights on an operating table I am panic stricken to observe. Physicians in white coats and masks surround the slab and peer down at me with a coldness only doctors can affect. I let out a howl – or perhaps I have been howling all along – and one of the doctors plunges a sixteen inch needle into my diaphragm.

It is very fuzzy, as though I were inside a storm of the kind you sometimes get when the picture suddenly burns out on your T.V. set. The smell of limes is in the air. And I cannot place its source. But the odor terrifies me. Then I notice Nurse Rose holding my right hand tight shut between her two immense manly palms.

"O, Mr. K," she says, "You gave us quite a start. You fainted among all those ladies."

"How ... how long was I out?"

"The better part of thirty minutes. How do you feel now?"

"I don't know. Did a physician inject me with something?"

"No. I'm sure."

"I feel wrecked."

"Well I'm going to prop you up with these nice pillows here," she says and begins arranging them behind my back and head to ease my disorientation.

"I need a glass of water. And can you give me my writing stuff over there?" I motion toward the nightstand with my head.

"Maybe you should be still a while, Michael?"

I find it awkward and disconcerting to hear her use my first name.

"Why did you call me Michael?"

"That is your name, isn't it?"

She hands me a plastic cup filled with water poured from a pitcher on the stand.

"But it's always by the first initial of my last name that you address me."

"So I made a little change."

"It's not the same. Am I in any danger of being seduced?"

"Don't flatter yourself Mr. K. I was only being motherly."

"I'm disappointed. I thought succour was at hand."

Nurse Rose gently places both the notebook and pen on the blanket over my crotch.

"Being horny is a good sign. It means you're recovering."

"Even though I fainted?" I ask weakly.

"I would not worry about that."

She turns and leaves, closing the thick door behind her. I stare listlessly in front of me a very long time before shutting the eaves of my wearied eyes as Tennyson has written somewhere.

Chapter Eight

Nurse Rose has taken me out to the general sitting area where I perch on a little easy chair with my *Thesaurus,* pen, and legal pad, noting a sigh or groan or cough from one patient or another. Since my encounter with the girls, I have had increased difficulty walking and I do not know why. And the literary pearls come to me in strands that reflect only silhouettes of death. It is because of these ideas that I dwell on Hitler.

I have a theory about Adolf. About how he developed. The alcoholic father. The beatings. The repeated traumas. The traumas must have triggered an hysterical symptom. An unconscious ability to throw his mind must have been generated as a compensatory mechanism to gather allies and converts to his side. A symptom of psychosis to convince them to turn against the evil father, the ogre who also abused his beloved mother and his siblings. So his unconscious mind led him to destroy the fatherland. That was his desire from the beginning. What additional torments might have been inflicted upon him as a choir boy? He may have been subjected more to the rituals of Caligula than of Christ. The evil priest. Like myself, he might have stood out like a sore thumb. People could hear him think. He must have drawn the attention of the Austro-Hungarian secret police. They would exacerbate his illness in order to stimulate patriotism, the name with which we glorify exaggerated expressions of our territorial imperative. But his desire to conquer must have been congenital.

Armies are not gathered. They are born. Only those apes survived who were killers, and in that prehistoric dawn of man's ascendancy – several millions of years ago – only the most efficient and effective killers were able to pass on their genes. Only those who effortlessly fought all the time – to whom the fame of martial glory meant the moon and stars, who loved war both real and feigned, who adored all the tools of battle more than a woman's body and endlessly polished stone axes and bone knives that ran through an enemy's belly or a foal as easily as wind through a field – were able to improve their tactical skills to full potential. Only such a creature would seek to integrate with other killers – through telepathy and conscious means – to mold an awesome strategic machine that could conquer the African savanna. Teams of sly hunters and brilliant soldiers that could stalk to its final

The Gangster Papalardo

breath any man or animal as easily as a farm boy shucks corn. One tribe against another as Old Man Mountain said. Fighting over limited resources in some plain or soggy panhandle or forest depth. Only when relaxed fully would nature allow them to fuck in peace, creating the optimum conditions for healthy offspring, for cunt and dick to be reunited in the thick muck of the beginning, the undifferentiated beginning. Oo la la. Spermatozoa and gamete in sensuous accord. After the tribal perimeter was secure. The foot soldier, the lieutenant, the little corporal, murderers all. Just so they could replicate. Senseless replication. Where does it all lead? No answers. Just process. All dictated by Nature. By the mighty call of the wild. And what part does religion play and culture play in this disgusting ooze? They are the warrior's protection, his psychological sword and shield. The booze from his canteen that anaesthetizes him from instinctive guilt and shame, those tribal taboos against raising his violent hand to other members of the clan whose tartan he wears. These furious groups, all living within a small space, must have resembled each other physically to such an extent that some means had to be forged to justify the murder of a natural brother. That brother had to be *demonized* if the group were to avoid starvation. The tribe had to protect from intruders those desirable limited resources at its command. There were not enough deer, horses, berries or orchards to serve the needs of everyone. Thus, they became the Chosen People or the One True Tribe or the Master Race and the outsider was a devil. The Moon God had ordained that you wear green stripes on your face and chest and back so that you could always tell a believer from an infidel or a barbarian. The spear of religion was pointed at every stranger and that instrument of death was a shield against the empathy which issues naturally from identification with another creature and the guilt which restrains us from allowing violent emotions to become violent actions. After killing the enemy, the shield would shut out entirely all feelings of remorse. Like displacement in dreams, an unconscious device I have chosen to call *replacement* tries to rule our waking life. It shifts emotions which are spontaneous, such as compassion, to the basement of one's mind, and puts religion in its place, so we are kept from seeing things too dreadful to recognize. Like the bits of brain and bone splattered when one swings an ax down on a child's head. Primitive man could not afford to realize what he was doing. It would endanger the clan. No one can be left alive to seek revenge.

The Gangster Papalardo

Chapter Nine

Victoria had returned to her husband for a two week trial. She had lost nearly forty pounds since we first met and looked good enough to bite.

"Shit. Everything's shit," she ranted, making a fuss with her hair, brushing it back with both hands and severely knotting a band in back to produce a ponytail. "It's just shit."

I toyed with my coke and finally said, "So Doctor Spaulding's not the fair haired boy of your dreams I guess."

"He doesn't love me. When he makes love to me, there's no feeling. It could just as well be another girl. Then he goes to sleep right away. Like a real shit."

"Excrement would seem to be the *motif* of today's *tableau*."

"*Tableau?*"

"Hogarth. *A Thief and his Doxy.*"

"You're kidding. There's no such Hogarth."

"I'm being creative."

"It's disgusting."
"I'll stop trying then."
" I'm referring to my problems. The pits."
"So talk about something else."
"I don't want to talk about anything else."
I began to wish I were eating alone.
"No foreplay," she said.
"No foreplay you say?"

She placed both elbows on the table and lowered her face into her cupped palms.

"No foreplay." With this refrain, she fell to weeping. I got up and put both my arms around her from the side as she rocked to and fro in her grief.

"I think your vagina's probably more delicious than the finest sugar. Let me have a taste," I implored. Laughing now, she pushed me away.

"You idiot."

"Just let me immerse my tongue in your fragrant juices a mere ten minutes and you'll feel like a million dollars the rest of the day."

"That's all you guys ever think about. Typical."

"What have *we* been talking about? I fall at your feet princess. Please let me lick out your cunt."

"You moron. Right here? Right now?"
"Why not?"

"People come in and out of here all the time. Are you insane? And he asks 'Why not?'" With slow, measured scorn, she shook her head.

The Gangster Papalardo

"Then you'll think about it?"
"We'll see."
"Perhaps today? After school?"
"I said I'd think about it. Not today in any case. Maybe never."
"But you'll think about it?"
"We'll see I said."
"Let's get back to husband Justin and foreplay. Why don't you suggest sixty-nine?"
"He refuses to have oral intercourse."
"You mean he never performs *cunnilingus*?"
"That's right."
"That's peculiar. You ever give him head?"
"No."
"Why not?"
"Because he doesn't think it's right for his wife to put his cock in her mouth."
"Not even now when you're both trying to get to the root of your problems?"
"Not even now."
"Then your husband's a really sick man."
"I guess so."
"There's nothing a man likes better than a blow job. It's the pink. Why not suggest a marriage counselor?"
"The pink?"
"We just saw a revival of *The Boys from Syracuse* off Broadway," I explain. She shakes her head at my stupidity.
"Well. So what about a marriage counselor?"

"He won't go. Damns psychiatry. Says it's witchcraft. Besides it costs too much. That's his *real* hang up. Rides the bus to Montefiore. Wants me to stop seeing my psychiatrist for the same reason."

"Are you going to quit?"

"I don't know. My shrink doesn't seem to be doing me much good. You're the only one who I can rely on to actually help now."

"You could switch doctors. What's your psychiatrist like?"

"He's an old idiot. Just says the usual things. Uh. Huh. Hum. And so on. Mike, this guy doesn't have a clue."

"How did you find him?"

"A friend."

I reflected that nothing meant anything. The idea was to avoid pain and suffering while alive. No one could do that very long. Only Tahitians perhaps, though modern times had pretty much erased those daydreams written on our collective imagination of one day joining Fletcher Christian's mutineers.

"I'm becoming Jewish," she said abruptly.

"Is there a rabbi involved in this or do you mean by some sort of subtle osmosis as in being too influenced by liberal ideas."

"I'm not kidding. I'm actually taking Hebrew lessons and Rabbi Hyman Gershwin is my teacher."

The Gangster Papalardo

"That old fake. I remember him pulling rebbetzin out of a skull cap on the Ed Sullivan Show."

"I'm serious. I will not allow tripe and shit to control my life."

"And when does the final conversion take place?"

"Sometime in June I think. Probably."

"Awesome."

"You don't believe me."

"I believe you all right. You know I had a passing thought just a moment ago. I would bet few people realize, had they cleverly bought beachfront property on Tahiti in the time of Gauguin, it would be worth nothing today. The entire island has been infested by rats and its lovely southern beaches are completely ruined."

"What is that supposed to mean?"

"Paradise lost. I've never found an answer that would prove the perfect antidote for what lice and life did to me."

"You don't believe in God, do you?"

"No."

"You don't believe in anything."

"And I don't believe in exchanging one set of handcuffs for another."

We argued some and it did not end in sex.

The Gangster Papalardo

Chapter Ten

Every time I approach the nurses' cubicle where they dispense the medication, I see the same three people, a cute teenage girl, a slim man in a green, faded sweater, and an older fellow with sparse gray hair and a pince-nez. For five days running they have been in the same place, dickering together in pantomime. What phase of my insanity are they supposed to represent? Clearly these bastards are elements of *Tresojos*. I am dead I think. When I look away, they move artfully into my view again. I know one is a patent attorney. I know because we were introduced. The other is a pharmacist I surmise, having overheard him conversing with a nurse one day about a bothersome lavatory experience and the effects of Thorazine on his bowels. I imagine the young lady must be a high school student. But why would they be told to playact before me like the three sisters in *Macbeth*? They want me to conclude that they are weird indeed, drawn from every aspect of life to haunt my

The Gangster Papalardo

waking hours and nettle my dreams. In short, the commonplace made frightening. Life turned into a nightmare. All coordinated.

And that is not all. I am required to go to group therapy. At each meeting, there are six or seven other medicated nuts. And the young lady teetering on graduation from high school. She always looks bright eyed and bushy tailed. Whenever my turn comes to speak – fool that I am – I goad the shrink detailed to our proceedings with my most vicious rhetoric regarding the medical profession, leaving my deadliest pus about psychiatry for last. The dull hack who is the attending physician usually lets the routine finish before asking any questions. But the adolescent *shmuck* springs up about half way through my *shtick*, keeping her eyes on me every minute and makes for the door. A broad hint she is going to report me to someone. So I become intimidated.

At what point in time I decided to take part in what became one of the most idiotic escapades in the broad wake of brainless things I call my life, it is difficult to say. But it began long after Victoria and I became close friends. Since people were chimpanzees – yea long before even that seminal development – gossip was the primate's coin of the realm for invigorating his normally dull existence. The fates have ordained that from such verbal leafing, both farce and tragedy should grow.

Since anyone who cared were those envious busybodies without lives, these schnooks began to make our *tête-à-têtes* vehicles for vicarious prickles. Hives of buzz-buzz droned whenever we tested such polls of public opinion, as these little shits comprised, by walking side by side down a hall, let's say, or across the student cafeteria. Many eyes of our colleagues present would be on us. Naturally, Victoria and I found it amusing, as who would not. Thus, we decided to give them something to die for and to talk about: the illusion of stupendous sex. Exaggerated hints of the most exquisite pleasures imaginable behind motel doors. Of course, nothing of the sort ever came close to initiation, except for that crazy offer on my part to perform *cunnilingus* in the teacher's lounge, next door to the staff dining hall – an offer rejected for reasons of propriety. Who could have envisioned the calamity that issued from such humble beginnings as I have described?

I noticed that those who seemed most annoyed at our spirited charade were Italians. The Doolittle staff boasted many of these. The dour kind who praised the dramatic Mussolini in private. To call them conservative would suggest that *chilly* is a fine description for the weather conditions in Knud Rasmussen Land during the twelve days of Christmas. They knew that Victoria was Italian it seems, a fact my 'love' had neglected to let me share. How does a man become intimate with a woman's dreams, her many sexual wounds, et al., and not discover her grandparents' ethnicity? If her married name is Spaulding, have no reason to care about national origins, and the game produces only ambiguous clues. Several weeks after we began our silly masquerade, she tells me that Luchesse is her maiden name; Rossary is the middle one. Victoria Rossary Luchesse, whose entire family on her mother's side moved from Kalambáka, Greece to Venice, Italy around 1910, where her mother was born eleven years later. The stern matriarch of her stock arrived in Manhattan circa 1922. Her father's half of the family hailed from *Reggio di Calabria*. And her cousin, a professor of anthropology at Duke University, had been able to trace their lineage in southern Italy back to the first Punic War. How pleased I am that we have forced many Italians in the school to think of me as an abusive fool who has broken up Victoria's happy marriage.

* * * * * * *

We were seated in my car one spring day in front of the brownstone where she rented a small apartment on the first floor. Fading light announced the evening's scented shade. There was the whiff of dogwood and the odor of baked bread from a small restaurant up the street. However, were these tender romantic tidings pressed with the vigor of Aphrodite in the flesh, it would not have pierced the thick armor of Victoria's self-absorption.

"I'm taking Valium," she said. "It doesn't seem to help much."

"Get a boyfriend," I said.

She looked out the side window. "That was my idea. But it hasn't worked. Why should anyone care about a skinny, ugly divorcée?"

"The divorcée part is attractive," I remarked. "Kinky sexual delights and exploits. The art of fucking personified by the sinful bitch who can't keep her legs together. Skinny and ugly get under the skin, however. But in fact, you are neither."

"None of the men in school are attracted to me."

"More than you think. But frazzled is your middle name. You always look at odds and ends. Understandably. You've been through shit."

"I hate Italian men," she said abruptly. She shuddered involuntarily, her torso trembling with a subterranean disgust that was terrible to watch. It reminded me of the kind of reflexive shaking you see in dogs when they emerge from cold water.

"How come?" I asked.

"They are greasy, imbecilic scum." She made a sound of loathing.

"So the men of Messina and other southern cities and climes are all condemned?" For some reason I presumed she meant those from Italy's boot.

The Gangster Papalardo

"That's right."

"The north too?"

"You really don't understand shit."

"Scatology is not my *forte*."

"Truthfully. Would you ever have anything to do with southern white trash?"

"No. But ..."

"Most Sicilians are garbage. Northern Italians won't even talk to them. They are primitive dunces. It's like trying to talk to some perverted savage from the Ozarks here in the United States."

"I thought you said you were of Calabrian vintage."

"Only my grandparents on my father's side. The maternal half are Venetian and Greek. I made a point of that," she said angrily.

"I grew up in a mixed neighborhood. Irish. Jews. Italians. In all the years I spent loitering on the corner with these guys, no one ever used the terms kike, wop or mick. We went to the same parties, the same schools, played baseball and basketball together. I never saw any difference between Jews and Italians. The Italians I knew looked like Jews. They had bad complexions, big noses and straight black or curly black hair. Their fathers were short, bald men like my father. They never committed any crimes. One Italian crony of mine became a dermatologist. The other I knew fairly well teaches English at a community college in Connecticut."

The Gangster Papalardo

"Assimilated," she said.

"What?"

"They have been assimilated. You are talking about Americans."

"They don't count?"

"You never met a *real* Italian."

"You mean a Sicilian?"

"A certain kind of Sicilian."

"They're all criminals?"

"Too many of them."

At that moment a cop car pulled up on the other side of the street, a little behind us. I turned my head towards it.

"Don't look at them," Victoria nervously urged. I returned my attention to the windshield. "If you look at them," she explained, "they think you feel guilty and will question you."

"A little Italian street lore?" I commented.

"That's right."

I didn't tell her that Jews, who had been persecuted by the constabulary for two thousand years, also knew these ploys.

The Gangster Papalardo

Chapter Eleven

Notebook Entry: September 27, 1969.
I am writing. Why did the fat man and the ladies effect me in such a bad way? They confirmed my worst fears. This thing exists. It exists objectively. And it is much like those strange, furtive creatures of mythology, the furies. They blend in perfectly with our daily sequence of existence that we do not notice: the dull routine, the everyday. Knots of bees that buzz and sting, against which this cranium of ours has built up armor. Witches, Shakespeare says or norns or whatever. But they only pierce the tough hide to shut down your brain when these criminals want to make you regress, to stop you or give you a cap and bells. Then they bite deep under the skin and trigger a sudden powerful gush – irresistibly powerful gush – of involuntary responses that lash through your system like shit through a goose, to quote George C. Scott's portrayal. You lose control of your voice, which begins to quiver like heat waves from tarmac

The Gangster Papalardo

when green quits suburban lawns for the cemetery brown of cremation. Your brain loses acquaintance with the brothers time and space who bid goodbye to order. Your visual sense wavers like a fat girl on a diet. Your hands tremble and it is as though someone has drawn a razor across your genitals. And your eyes begin to tear. Noises swell and subside, like the voices Bogey might hear coming out of being sandbagged in a film noir. Your teeth chatter uncontrollably, making those rapid little clicking sounds associated with Fred Astaire doing a tap dance. Anyone you meet might take you for an idiot, which is the entire point. If you have an important meeting to attend, you will meet only failure, and it *will* change your life.

But if buzz buzz buzz does not exist, then their techniques do not exist, and if their techniques do not exist, then their crimes never took place. And if their 'crimes' are only fabrications, then anyone who insists on their reality is either an alien *agent provocateur* degrading the authorities or insane. And we all know what happens to people who are mad. They grow progressively worse until they commit suicide or have an accident or are taken away "for their own good" by the kind of person who removes the poor clerk from the party at the end of Dostoevski's *The Double*.

And if these norns are operating to punish people, then the people whom they punish deserve their fate. And the man or woman who dares to

The Gangster Papalardo

speak about buzz buzz buzz is a traitor who wants to explain how the good and great Lords of the Earth are driving people insane and inducing individuals such as Lee Harvey Oswald to murder irresponsible profligates like Jack Kennedy or are encouraging men like Sirhan Sirhan to kill degenerate scum such as Robert Kennedy. The dog who speaks of 'the furies' must be dealt with swiftly and must be dealt with harshly. Death to traitors. *Reich* security is endangered. For reasons of prudence, no one says anything. If these heroic fellows blow up the world, we will all die together, and if by some extraordinary circumstance we avoid universal death, then you will remain among the living.

Gossip and whispering campaigns cannot be accepted as the security of the nation. These are the most notorious, noisome, and commonplace pieces of equipment in the totalitarian's bag of dirty tricks, and have been with us since we were knee high to the rare lion monkey of Brazil. The tamarin can drive you mad with its chatter if it chooses to do so. Analysis of such torment is treason only to an idiot, a criminal, a Nazi, a traitor or a Communist. It is by convincing the average, naïve citizen that cackle is the nation's first line of defense that the man on the street is relieved of his first amendment rights, his coveted faith in the firm nature of the real estate beneath his feet, and in the laws of justice that Professor Smith maintains are the backbone of a stable economy. When villains feel their power slipping, they manufacture crises so that they can frighten the little man into sacrificing fact for rhetoric and his liberty for the safety of 'temporary' infringements on those sacred amendments the brigands Washington, Jefferson, and Franklin forged as a safeguard against tyranny. Did the ladies attack me because of what I said to Rathbone? Did the ladies attack me at all?

Why are the Italians always involved? This 'thing' was created in the reign of Tiberius to control insurgent or merely insulting minorities such as Jews, early Christians, Brits, Germans, etc. The authorities became Catholic. The Germans invaded eventually and the Brits went home. Only those Christ killing Jews were left for snitches to thwart, using evil Sejanus *buzz buzz buzz*. The Hebrew Sigmund Freud arrives. *The Interpretation of Dreams* promises to turn mayflies into eagles, insightful and masterful. They no longer respond with their ancient anxieties. Herr Doctor's fervent first pupils psychoanalyze their own dreams. The Austro-Hungarian authorities get annoyed at their calm. So they decide to imitate those awful towering distortions that adorn the raiments of sleep and stir in their victims all the symptoms of psychosis found in the waking hours of crazy people. That hall of horrors with its hysteria. The psychiatrists *know* it must come from outside. The snitches whisper in their ears that it is the thought

The Gangster Papalardo

police and murder them as traitors to the realm. They committed suicide! Six psychoanalysts and a psychologist. All disciples of Freud in the early 20th century. Not a good recommendation for psychoanalysis to the general public. These people were set up, just as I am being set up. They seem to be after anyone who gains control over his or her unconscious mind. Threats to the stumbling *status quo* made up of stupid or ignorant or vicious or racist or power hungry totalitarians. How many other people were having their souls poisoned by The Eye in this madhouse? I had seen some peculiar things here. But I would venture to guess no one save Michael was being picked on with so much vigor. The minions of The Eye are legion, drawn from every trade and profession, and they are ubiquitous.

In the afternoon my wife and children arrive. My son Saul and my daughter Darlene are five and six. They are much more drenched with compassion for their suffering father than my skeptical wife who regards my torment as a species of irresponsibility. The whore.

"When are you coming home Poppy," Saul softly purrs, taking my hand. I break down in tears. Soon everyone is in tears, except Dee who observes her spouse and brood inscrutably.

"Come upstairs," I say. Sexual intercourse is in my mind. I am so disturbed that fucking my own wife presents itself as a relief.

"The children are not allowed," she parries, guessing my intentions.

"We can leave them at the nurses' station. 'Visiting Parent Services' it says." I motion toward the sign with my head.

We go upstairs and I bring Dee to my room. When we get inside, I ask her for a blow job. But she refuses. I beg her desperately to at least afford me the kindness of a hand job or a quickie. For my trouble, I am shoved. She does not understand the situation. I take her hand and begin to sketch letters on her palm. I mean to tell her that they are here. They induced Oswald to murder the President and Sirhan Sirhan to kill Bobby and the wall directly over the headboard of my bed hides a listening device and an eye which follows my every movement. But she snatches her hand away before I even can trace the third word and loudly hisses "You had better get your shit together and get out of here. You are destroying your children." She begins to weep.

"But you don't understand," I implore, whispering and trying to shush her. Dee will not listen and goes to the door, pulling it back and walking out into the corridor.

I am on my way to my lawyer for the third time in as many weeks. I have called him at least ten times in the last fourteen days. There is nothing.

The Gangster Papalardo

He has a good laugh each time, I am sure. He takes my anxieties very lightly.

His offices are located on the upper east side, which offers some gray hint of staid and historic stability. The buildings date from eighteen ninety to nineteen twenty-nine. All the turmoil of modern life – the hate, the surreal obsessions, the terror, evil run amok – are from another era. After the crash, when belly rebellion rocked the universe. How could anything bad happen on 93rd Street?

It is a long office of polished wood. The polished wood suggests wisdom and light. A place where grave issues are suited to gray minds that pursue, grasp, brand, and weigh the legal fouls that come their way. Their prey released finally to roost in dusty courts where they founder or share a victory with some wealthy client. I am not wealthy. Israel David Harbinger comes recommended by my mother. He was my father's bridge partner for the last twenty years of Simon Kapmarczyk's life and bid the last hand with him up to a seven no trump grand slam, the point at which dear old dad suffered his fatal stroke.

The receptionist tells me to take a seat. Mr. Harbinger was with a client. I scan legalistic issues in quarterly publications and wait. Eventually, Israel Harbinger emerges with a wrinkled lady of some vintage on his arm, who reels slightly like a leaky boat, as they babble in mock delight at some garbled witticism the senile old bag out of habit repeats on her yearly visit to the lawyers. Harbinger diplomatically smiles and laughs it up. But that is just my take on the scene I glimpse at the end of the long corridor leading to Harbinger's door. If truth be told, at that distance, I cannot hear a thing.

The octogenarian witch hobbles by with her knobby shillelagh digging up the rug on one side. Zero Mostel supports in courtly style her other wing as they progress toward the door.

He returns to where I am sitting, looks down at me with a mixture of professional dignity and compassion, hooks his left arm behind his back and meshes his right hand with mine in a handshake to affirm his commitment to solving my set of absurd, godforsaken little problems.

"How have you been, Michael?" says he.

"Fine. And you, sir?" I rise from the couch, still clutching his hand, urgently and effectively suppressing a ferocious desire to address him as Poldy Bloom.

"Can't complain," he smiles, folksy now. "How's your mother?"

"Good. She's well."

"Let's go inside," Harbinger says, touching my left shoulder. He inclines his head, peering at me curiously, as one might peer at a bug.

There are lines of dark texts athwart oaken shelves on every wall. The shades of the windows have been drawn shut. The high ceiling of the room adds to the signs of gloomy contemplation borne on

The Gangster Papalardo

the must of lawyerly vapor. Two portraits adorn the area above Harbinger's desk, and neither looks as though its prototype had ever made love.

Harbinger shuffles some papers and commences to speak. "Mike, don't say anything until I am through. You know I am committed in every respect to helping you. I mean more than just within my compass as a lawyer, but as a human being. Your father – God rest his soul – and your dear mother, have for nearly forty years been my closest friends. I tell you this in the most fond hope and expectation that my words will serve to quell the fears you've erected in relationship to the matters we've broached. I don't mind saying your mother has been generous as to my troubles on your behalf. No effort has been spared." Now he bends his face toward me across the desk. "Very extensive inquiries have been made throughout the justice system at every level of federal and state bureaus, down to the local departments. No stone has been left unturned. No one, *no one* is after you. You are not a lowlife. You are not under any kind of political surveillance. No one is investigating you. I have spent hours in conversation with every single head of department. Your name is not on their list. It is like being to the Mayo Clinic. You have a clean bill of health. Pristine. A clean bill of health. Don't you understand? You have been to the legal Mayo Clinic. And there is nothing wrong."

"So there's ... nothing wrong," I mumble.

"Nothing amiss." I rub my chin with a thumb and index finger.

"Now will you just fix your attention elsewhere. Start a hobby. Learn to enjoy life." Harbinger smiles at me full face and with crinkly slitted eyes.

"Only some phase of life I'm passing through," I suggest.

"That's right."

"Well look," I begin, fumbling for the proper words – the precise verbs, the right syntax – which casually elude me, prod their way back again past slithering lexicons and fade once more along the edge of the ragged horizon that rings my consciousness. "Mr. Harbinger, I, uh...haven't told you the whole truth. There are some things about the hospital where I am that are weird. Strange things...happening."

"Yes," the lawyer remarks, a tired note of gnarly contempt creeping into his voice.

"Mr. Harbinger, there are people there...I don't know how to put it...who seem...who...I don't know quite how to put it. That coordinate their efforts...who seem, well...carefully rehearsed."

"You're imagining things," Harbinger says.

"No, I'm not. I don't think so. They really suggest...they work for our Orwellian thought police." My words appear suddenly to have gotten the lawyer's attention. He erupts from his chair,

The Gangster Papalardo

eyes bulging.

"No," he says. "It's impossible," all the while making erasing gestures, as he fixes his eyes on the wall above my head.

"Mr. Harbinger. Please. We all know the thought police piss on our rights. ..."

"An Italian girl did this to you," he says, banging a fist on his desk. "Am I right?"

"Yes. ...But ..."

Harbinger crashes his fist again on the desk. "Italian girl," he shouts at an ill defined area some - place above my head. "Italian girl."

"How did ..." I am about to ask the lawyer how he knew it was an Italian girl who had stirred up this mess, but he interrupts me.

"You were lovers?" Israel Harbinger asks.

"No."

"Very close friends?"

"Yes. Very good friends."

"She works with you in the same department at your high school," he states.

"Yes."

"Her name."

"Victoria Spaulding."

"Tell me. When you first had this 'nervous breakdown' which landed you in the hospital, were you on the way to see your psychiatrist?"

"Yes."

"Is he associated with the hospital you're in?"

"Yes. The head of psychiatry."

"Did you notice you were being tailed by some tough looking characters on your way to the hospital? I mean slick hair, seedy appearance. People one might have thought of as gangsters perhaps?"

"Yes. That happened."

"And did they go out of their way to indicate they were tailing you."

"Yes. They did. Came right up either side of me and deliberately brushed against my arms."

"Yes. Of course," Harbinger says. "Her name again."

"Victoria Spaulding. She has a psychosis and responds to the word *schizoid* by almost fainting." Harbinger says nothing to this. He gets up from behind his desk and comes toward me with his right hand extended. He is smiling confidently. I get up and we shake. He places his left hand on my shoulder and guides me toward the door of his office. As I pass through into the corridor, the lawyer says, "Stop worrying. Go home and watch television."

"I'm still in the asylum," I remind him.

The Gangster Papalardo

Chapter Twelve

In the lovely month of May, we staged our donnybrook. Quite tritely, drear is man's foremost spiritual demon. Id, ego, libido, and spite perform a quadrille as the ancient proverb says, so let us settle on the particulars of this outrage – an outrage we shall find blessed with all an imp of the perverse ever designed for human torment.

We were seated in Romalla's Pizzeria, near the school. Four of us. Norman Toby, the boyfriend of Victoria's earnest little pal Margie Snodgrass, Victoria and mental health's poster boy, yours truly.

The conversation was desultory, as the pulp fiction *auteurs* say. And for no reason that will ever make sense, while eating a giant cannoli, I made a claw of my right hand and distorted my face into a Quasimodo-type grimace aimed at the ever unstable and graceful Victoria.

Victoria made believe she had not seen my weird contortion. But her eyes skittered away in a panic dance of hot pursuit after the clowns of someplace else. It shocked the Snodgrass woman and phased her main squeeze. I followed up this idiocy by abruptly rising, headed for the cashier's counter where I deftly slid the check and appropriate amount to the fat lady working the register. As I passed out the door onto Grant Boulevard, I could imagine her friend Margie advising Victoria that she could not allow me to get away with such a performance.

For the better part of the next four weeks, Margie Snodgrass, Victoria, and their friends gave me the old silent treatment, tweaked my Jewish paranoia with various barbs, and generally nettled the bland course of my inane existence. All of which I furtively encouraged. It helped to foment in the senseless minds of these tarts the erroneous idea planted by the Spaulding woman and myself of our torrid liaison. So I cultivated a whimsical melancholy, one designed to foreshadow the baffled Victoria's *rapprochment** with the penitent Michael.

"You must forgive me for my grotesque behavior some weeks ago," I began when I had gotten her alone. "You know we all do stupid things from time to time. Then again it might be out of a thwarted desire to fuck you." I gave her my

---

*Another slip of the pen. Significantly, the **foreign** word, rapprochement, is misspelled. Harmonious adjustments are indeed foreign to this patient's nature. – M. W.

The Gangster Papalardo

most practiced Raskalnikov stare, intended to intimate my concern and to boast the intensity of my desire.

"You have a strange way of expressing affection," she reflected. "But you're right. We all do act like assholes from time to time. I won't wreck our faux relationship over that shit. We would foil the gallery. Just don't let it happen again."

"O no. I promise. You can rest assured. Just sometimes I get a bit schizoid and ... ." At the issue of the word *schizoid* from my lips, she let out a hiss, gripping her temples between her polished fingernails, then closed her eyes and rocked side to side.

"Easy," I said, touching her right knee. She posed rigidly a moment in mid dither.

"What's wrong?" I said.

"O God. Don't use that word ever again," half commanded and half pled the disturbed woman.

"What word?"

"The one you just used referring to a psychosis."

"I understand."

"It's a nail right through the center of my head. I almost faint every time I hear that word."

It was not unnatural for me to call her after

this *tête-à-tête*. We were always speaking to one another. True, school was over and there had been no reference on either side to seeing each other during the summer break. But neither had we shut the door to an occasional rendez-vous in those broiling months. My panting breast craved the cooling possibility of thermal raising love to ease the noisome weight of one hundred degrees mingled with the savage effluvium shouting from huge metal cans left overflowing by a strike of the garbagemen's union. So I called her and she told me to come over. I even bought a bottle of wine for our tryst.

    Now, dear reader, as one of Dostoevski's characters might say, I must pause and give you some sort of explanation of why I am unable to dramatize this part of my little story. To put it in the most trite terms my smallish imagination can conjure on momentary notice, it is the Beethovian knock upon the door of my tiresome existence. If this event had never taken place, I like to think destiny had in store for me a less terrifying experience than has been the case. It is evolution's design that we take humiliating episodes and transform them into glorious art. Our fancy saves us from the appropriate depression which might lead to suicide. Instead of Fitzgerald presenting the case history of a pathological gangster attempting to transform reality by brute force, we get *The Great Gatsby*. Instead of Jay Gatz putting a bullet hole

The Gangster Papalardo

through Tom Buchanan's heart, we have a great poet unconsciously trying to banish time à la *The Psychopathology of Everyday Life*. "Luckily the clock took this moment to tilt dangerously at the pressure of his head, etc." Yes, I memorized those lines. Not because I think I am the immortal Fitzgerald or his wonderful creation, but because I know I am Charlie Chaplin in *The Great Dictator,* the pathetic Jew from one of Malamud's fictions. I too want to banish time. The problem of course is greater and more universal than my suffering. Do we really want to know what tree shrew insecurities and unofficial manipulations of the public mind made MacArthur MacArthur or Winston Churchill Winston Churchill? It would seem we are only willing to face the disgusting bathroom and bedroom traumas of people who have truly turned out poorly, the current revealed cannibal or serial killer. If our magnificent killers, our Oscars of the Waldorf one might say, carved well and at the appropriate time, sublimating their murderous natures strictly in the interests of mankind and the state, we do not want to know any of their dirty little secrets. It would defeat the purpose of presenting them as marble busts for the younger generation to emulate. Those Jungian packages of chemistry that protect the territory and allow the group to endure must themselves be protected from the magnifying glass of scientific inspection. What congenital gifts, what *good fortune*, what *lucky* social standing made Marlborough Marlborough instead of the Yorkshire Strangler? And could that very strangler have become the idol of British children with a single fortuitous roll of the fatal bones?

So I knocked upon the door. And she opened it, pleasantly attired. An alluring dress. "I have bought you a gift," I said. "Come in," she motioned, smiling. In retrospect, although I was not conscious of it at the time, had she not been Italian, I probably would have fairly raped her at the outset. With her permission of course. And she would have enjoyed it too. But we got into a conversation about literature instead. And this led to a question about why she and her friends had spread stories about me, which she denied. Then she accused me of not liking her because she was Italian – the furthest thing from my mind. I told her the allegation was ridiculous. She told me to get out. I said I was just leaving. She opened the door and demanded I remove myself from James Doolittle High School, although not quite in the polite terms I have suggested. I shot back, "No. You get out." "We'll see," she said, and added "You filthy bastard." I countered with "Fuck you, you dirty bitch." Out of the corner of my eye, I noticed her holding open her door with one foot as she watched me walk up the street. So I turned and yelled, "O yeah. I poisoned the wine, so you better watch out." Charlie Brown and Lucy, *hors d'ici!* Straight out of a James

The Gangster Papalardo

Thurber story one would imagine. And there it should have ended. But of course it did not.

Five days later I found myself at the headquarters of district 12, along with fifteen other angry teachers whom the central board had assigned to Horace Witherspoon Junior High. Apparently, our summer positions had been given to people selected by the recently empowered local board of education. We contacted the UFT and waited for someone to help us.

Every school day we had to clock in by 8:00 a.m. and could not leave until 2:20. We sat and talked and griped.

Tuesday of the second week, Arturo Martabano showed up. Another teacher who had been thrown out by the local board. And at about this time, the attitude of my colleagues began to change toward me. In vague ways. Disturbing little things. Above all I sensed something sneaking past me.

One day, two of the female teachers in our group asked me to drive them to Pelham Parkway, which was along the route I motored in routinely to get home. When I stopped the car to let them out, they both asked me at once, in stumbling chorus, if there was someone in the English department at Doolittle I confided in on a regular basis.

"What?" I said. It was an odd question.

"There's someone in the English department I knew years ago," the one called June offered.

"And when you were talking this afternoon to Arturo on the subject of soul mates, your description of this individual brought her to mind, and I need to see her about a project I am involved with."

"What's her name?" I asked.

"You know I don't recall. But I am trying to remember. She was Italian if I'm not mistaken."

"Victoria Spaulding?"

"Are you close to her?"

"Yes. We're good friends."

"I'm nearly certain that's the lady. Would you have her phone number and address handy?"

"Yeah. Do you want them?"

"Yes. That would be good of you."

I fished a piece of paper out of my wallet and let her copy down the numbers. Had this exchange of information not taken place, in retrospect I probably would have been assassinated last summer.

Some forty-three teachers had been excessed from Doolittle in June. Another five or six had probably been notified by mail during the vacation months, which was not unusual in the New York City Public School System. Ordinarily these people would have been sent their checks in September or told to pick them up at their new school the first day of work. Had I been transferred during the summer, I would never have connected this with my final conversation with Victoria. And I would likely not

The Gangster Papalardo

have given her another thought for the remainder of my days on earth. Chances are, the evil scum who were behind what ensued, realized this and had the power to avoid the catastrophe which developed.

When the fall semester began, Victoria Spaulding was not foremost in my autumnal thoughts, except for an occasional glance. The lot used for teacher parking was ghostly. My ancient car was among the first to arrive and the empty numbered spots guided my somber curiosity around whirling ideas of time, rather than the lost labors of lust. Had I gotten the hour wrong we were to gather? What anvil struck among the gods had suddenly announced the orchestration of my doom? I was mildly perturbed.

The side doors were both locked, so I was forced toward the front portal of the battered edifice. And there I saw George Shapiro, the confidante with whom I sometimes ate lunch.

"George, my good fellow," I cawed, climbing the stairs.

"Hello Mike," he said with a most worried air.

"Well, we're back and the entrances are blocked. Like the gates of heaven itself to Lucifer and his band." Shapiro did not smile at my jest. His attitude offered me the same consolation as a mild rebuke, not unlike the empty parking lot.

"We're early," he said.

"Feel like having some coffee?"

"Sure," he agreed.

So we went up the street to the doughnut shop.

"How was your summer?" I asked when we were seated.

"Very good," he said softly.

He was too serious, and his serious tone made me anxious. There was something wrong.

"Go anyplace?"

"We have a place up in Maine. My wife and I and the kids spent August up there."

The waitress came over and we ordered Danish pastry and coffee.

"Get in any fishing?" I inquired.

"Bass and perch. A few trout," Shapiro answered glumly. "And you?"

"We went to a place called Solway House in upstate New York with some friends."

"Did you have a good time?"

"It was alright."

There was something about the deadness of the conversation that alarmed me. Shapiro looked plainly worried. And he avoided looking me in the eye.

When we went back, the doors were open and most of the other teachers had punched in. Some were milling around, glad-handing and hugging in the area hunched between the principal's office and the secretarial pool. I saw Victoria there, looking timid in the circle of her friends, which

The Gangster Papalardo

included four other ladies. I made believe they didn't exist. But as I slid by this buzzing knot of females, it occurred to me that being pleasant does not take an exceptional effort. *Quoi qu'il en soit,* the notion fell on deaf ears.

"Let's make him friendly," I heard the Snodgrass woman snarl. My back was to them and the voice of another damoiselle reached my ears. "Don't have a hand in this. These things lead to murder." It was eerie and curious, like the fading refrain of a murmur in a dream.

"Does the staff meet in the p.m. or this morning?" Nick Flynn asked as I went by. I shrugged.

The acrid smell of a powerful cleaning solvent stung my nose and lungs at the entrance to the first floor corridor. Fingers of odor crept down my throat. A throng of teachers bobbed down the hall toward the elevator like empty bottles in a stream. When they passed the bathroom, some of the men hesitated, as though by prearrangement, and a few entered. I often stopped there myself before going up. Gaining control of my bladder, however, on this occasion, was not difficult, noting the crowd that would be in three lines lurching toward the *pissoirs*. Four or five milled about the left side of the shithouse, as though ruminating whether to ascend or stand. Stand at the urinals that is. So to avoid this strangely uncomfortable situation, I took the stairs.

The odor of cleaning solvent grew stronger. And by the time I reached the third floor, my eyes were tearing slightly. I wiped away the moisture with a soiled handkerchief.

Why no one else was about I could not say. My nervousness made me feel isolated and I became panicky, as one might in a nightmare. An eerie light played upon the polished corridor floor from the huge windows at the end of the hall. And the stench from the ingredients used to wash the surfaces became all I could bear. The fumes were like those you smelled constantly in a hospital. *A hospital.* In my mind I repeated the phrase. It stuck and echoed in my head. Then Norman Toby, the boyfriend of the Snodgrass woman, abruptly appeared.

"Norman," I said. "Am I glad to see you. Nobody is here. It's like a tomb. Where the hell is everyone?" And I laughed. He tilted his face to the side and stared. I felt him look at me as though my flesh had melted in front of his eyes.

"They're in the auditorium," he finally replied, and we began walking in that direction.

"Did you get any notice? And that goddamned odor is enough to drive anyone crazy," I commented. Toby took a step away from me, as if deliberately drawing a line between us.

"It was posted above the clock."

The third floor auditorium had seen better days as the library, which was now located on the

The Gangster Papalardo

second floor. No explanation to the teaching staff was ever given for these queerly bold readjustments. The original auditorium on the first floor was now used only to seat students coming off their heroin shots. To address a crowd of supervisors and teachers in such a place must have graduated into some sort of taboo of awful dimensions, intimating an educational failure so immense, it could not be faced. So the staff meetings were elevated above the problem, as though to say the horror had no substance.

The staff began to trickle into the vast room two floors above the "non-existent" monster – now a mere shade – that would fast become a nodding beast when the student body arrived two days hence. The hum of conversation died when the principal and his attendants took center stage. His speech fumbled on. A pause to rinse his mouth with a hurried swallow of water half way through. Then he continued another thirty minutes. At last the man fought off an angry hive of embarrassing questions designed by a few deans to sting his pride. Finally we were dismissed.

In the entire quarter hour that preceded this insipid and deadly orientation, everyone close by treated me as though I were suffering from a contagion that rendered my form invisible. I tried to address by name a woman I knew casually, Cybelle Longfellow, but she managed to ignore me. My panic grew. Some people were going for coffee, and

I clung to this group, allowing their wake to pull me down the stairs and along the street. By the time we arrived at the café, my head felt as though it were being ripped from my neck, as if at any moment it would be sent floating into the rumbling fans slowly turning along the shit colored ceiling. I grabbed an empty glass from an uncleared table and flung it.

"This must stop," I shouted. Immediately, everyone in the narrow shop turned his or her eyes toward me. "I know what is going on," I bellowed. George Shapiro got up from one of the tables and gently put his arm around my shoulders.

"Mike," he said. "You're not feeling well. Let's go outside."

I allowed myself to be guided toward the exit. When we got outside, Shapiro motioned me to keep quiet.

"I'm parked nearby. Let's drive around and talk. My car is a block away."

"What's wrong?" he asked when we were inside his station wagon.

"The whole place is orchestrated against me," I answered in a frenzy.

"Take it easy. You're imagining things," he said. "Let's drive around a little and mull it over."

Shapiro edged out of his space and headed down Webster Avenue toward the North Bronx. He drove slowly.

"Is everything alright at home?" he inquired, with false calm.

The Gangster Papalardo

"Yes," I answered.

"What's going on here?"

"I don't know. The whole place seems hostile. Orchestrated against me," I insisted.

"Were you fooling around with one of the co-eds"?

"No. I swear. Nothing like that."

He remained silent for some time. Then he made a turn up a side street to go around the block and head back toward the school.

"Whatever you do, don't crack up. Keep control of yourself. Are you able to do that?"

"I'm alright," I exploded suddenly. "Check me out." I was not sure why I said this, but the episode with passing the men's room earlier came to mind. A ghastly idea that they were saying something about my genitals occurred to me.

"Don't crack up," he warned tensely. "Don't throw the whole thing away. You understand?"

"I understand. I'll control myself."

When we got back to the building, Shapiro parked the car again in its old spot, and we went inside. As we passed through the entrance, Nick Flynn came up to us and said, "The afternoon orientation has been cancelled. Some information sheets and booklets haven't arrived from Livingston Street, so we're going to hold the rest of the shit at 8:30 tomorrow morning in the auditorium upstairs. Got that? And that's when we'll get our paychecks. Tomorrow morning. We can clock out in about five minutes." Then he walked away.

We arrived at the area where the teachers' mailboxes were located, between the principal's office and the secretarial pool. The place where I had first seen Victoria that morning.

I looked in my mailbox and there was a brief greeting to the teachers printed on xerox paper. I threw it into the nearest wastepaper basket.

I sat down at one of the tables. Victoria and her friends were there again and I stared at them. If I hadn't been such a *poseur*, I would never have continued with my stupid act. But I decided to play the tragic lover one more time. I placed a hand on either side of my face and watched Victoria's expression balefully. She had been looking at me with a depressed cast over her features. Then she made a movement toward me. But the Snodgrass woman grabbed her shoulder and hissed, "Don't go near him."

"O Victoria," I said, forcing crocodile tears into my eyes. The Snodgrass woman guided Victoria toward me by one firmly gripped elbow. Victoria stood next to her, some ten feet away, wearing a shocked and sorrowful look.

"She called The Eye," Snodgrass enunciated firmly. I felt as though someone had thrown a pail of ice water in my face. And I realized suddenly, if it were true, then everything I had experienced that morning might have been induced, might have been premeditated. It was as though the hand of death had been irrevocably closed around my throat. I burst into real tears and brushed them away from my face with the backs of my hands as I had seen my five year old son do. And with an awful relevance, I saw myself as the protagonist at the end of *The Double*. Then I got up and fled the place, hurried through the hall to the entrance, and nearly ran down the stone stairs of the school. I saw George Shapiro racing after me out of the corner of my eye. He grabbed me by the arm at the bottom of the steps and said, "Who did this to you?" He was angry and terribly upset.

"Victoria Spaulding," I said.

"Are you going to throw your life away for a cunt? A dirty, stupid little cunt?"

"I can't help it," I said. A look of rage passed over his face. As he turned to go, I added, "She has a psychosis and responds to the word 'schizoid' by almost fainting."

He seemed annoyed by this information. And before I could add that Margie Snodgrass had a hand in all this, he dashed back up the stairs and into the building.

I got my car. When I closed the door, I remained for a few minutes behind the wheel, weeping uncontrollably. Why this crying jag enveloped me like a cloud was not something I could fathom. An image of April had flashed through my mind when the Snodgrass woman had grabbed Victoria's shoulder, keeping some kindly gesture from being expressed. It was several months before I could adequately analyze how this awful gust of tears had swept away the magical Tarot cards, each picture delicately balanced against another, that had been my castle.

I drove home. No one was there. So I drove down to Manhattan to see Rathbone. He had been my psychiatrist for several months. I parked my car in a garage and started walking the four blocks toward his office. Two strange looking men began stalking me. And they made no pretense of disguising the fact. They could have been thugs from their appearance. Both had five o'clock shadows, with slicked back hair and ten dollar suits. I slowed down, hoping they would go by. They caught up and made sure they brushed against me as they passed, one on either side. Then they stopped at a display window. I crossed the street and they followed. My panic grew, and as I got half a block from the hospital, these men evaporated. Gone. Like a puff of wind.

On my insistence that it was an emergency, I got to see Rathbone within half an hour. My hysteria caused him to frown and rub his beard. He would not admit me unless it was on a voluntary basis, which would allow me to go and come as I chose and to discharge myself permanently when I liked. This is how I came to be a patient in the Louis C. Furr pavilion of Godspell Hospital.

Chapter Thirteen

My first full day in the lunatic asylum, I rose early and breakfasted at a little table, sitting opposite an old lady. We did not speak. There was hardly any conversation at all in the small dining room. Each patient was doing a fair imitation of a cigar store Indian, nearly immobile and taciturn. I was uncomfortable with them. I finished hurriedly, and lined up with the other mad people at the nurses' station to receive a regimen of pills, which included Thorazine.

It is after I had taken my medicine that I first encountered the man in the yellow bathrobe. He had been watching me intently. Just watching. I do not know why I was targeted for such observation, but it frightened me, and in order to avoid him, I went into the sitting room.

It was an immense room by the standards of the place, with several murals and paintings hanging on the walls. There were couches, easy chairs, wooden chairs, and wicker rocking chairs strewn about the area in no particular order. On a long, black, central table were ashtrays and magazines. A television was playing, but no one seemed to be watching. I went over to one of the couches and began to watch a morning show that was in progress. Some actor was being interviewed. Abruptly, the man being questioned leaned forward and looked at me with bulging eyes. "Schizoid women are fascinating," he said quite emphatically. I jerked my head back in panic. Then the actor remarked, "I believe Lady Macbeth should be played as a schizoid personality. The ambitious fiend wrestling with a conventional woman of conscience. Two distinct people."

    I got up from the couch and turned toward the entranceway of the room. *My God,* I thought, *he was speaking directly to me. But how is that possible? I must really be going insane? But is it possible? An organization like **Tresojos** could easily induce an actor to say such a thing, a seemingly harmless sort of cooperation. He might be one of their snitches, which would obligate him to cooperate. But how could they coordinate such an effort? Someone here making a telephone call to the studio? The man in the yellow bathrobe, perhaps? Simulate the symptoms of paranoia to evoke all the anxiety of real paranoia. Or was it coincidence, perhaps a kind of synchronicity?* I was trembling, and began to shuffle rather than walk across the enormous room. *But why should they be interested* *in me? What have I done? How could they care enough about me to mount an investigation of this kind?* Then I remembered someone remarking that the reputations of people in power were built on bullshit. They took care of a thousand little things very well, but never touched the big problems. Which helped our enemies. Like a man playing chess who becomes obsessed with chasing an opponent's pawn, so the moment he takes it from the board, the other man checkmates him.

As I left the sitting room, I noticed three people in conversation. They appeared to be mouthing their words. Not a sound came from them. Two men and a young woman. And for a reason not clear to me then, I thought, *These people murdered the President of the United States. I'm a dead man.*

Chapter Fourteen

Why hadn't April Evesin and I stayed together? I had a nervous breakdown. No, not like the present one, but not too different either. Some three weeks or so after April confided in me her story about the rape, I began to fall apart. In retrospect – I infer from vague memories – I was being neutered, but did not realize it at the time. It was the subtle kind of harassment that gets under your skin and makes you lend your mind to paranoid fantasies. The process is gradual. But I was particularly vulnerable to this horrid form of annoyance because her ordeal reminded me of an ordeal of my own. I had been sexually traumatized and was unable to face the full impact of the causative incident, the details of which I suppressed – even from myself.

Every time I met with April or just spoke to her on the phone, I was overcome by grief. Sometimes I wept for eighteen hours at a time. I wept not only out of self pity – I could not explain at the time why I was breaking down – but out of

The Gangster Papalardo

the most profound compassion for this beautiful creature whose love I had won. I identified with her so strongly, even more strongly after she told me about Papalardo, that my existence became nothing but tears. The details and effect of my own awful experience pressed increasingly upon my mind and I found it impossible to hold back the consciousness of this nightmare. So I did the only thing I could to escape recognizing my problem. I broke off with April.

Looking back, I remember my father being incessantly harassed. My own experiences have made me understand his predicament. He might have been alright if they had left him alone. And I certainly would have been alright if they had left me alone. Apparently these imbeciles deliberately traumatize you at one stage of your existence in preparation for making an example of you five or ten years hence. The minions of *Tresojos* induce the very neuroses and **crimes** they then pretend to discover. They want a powerful reaction. And this brings back to me the memory of other horrors from the past.

No American should be harassed. No citizen should have his privacy invaded. No American should be singled out and assassinated. From the perspective of 1969, I recall incidents that took place more than twenty years ago when I was a child.

It was a Saturday afternoon around 12:00

The Gangster Papalardo

noon. Summertime. Everyone was at home. My sister had tuned in a pop music program on the radio. Suddenly the disk jockey said, "Here is our friend again. Now we take you live to his apartment. There is a Sicilian gentleman climbing up the fire escape. ... Now he is climbing into our friend's open window. ... He has a very long knife in his hand." Then we heard a young man scream, his voice getting higher and higher. "No. No. O my God, no. ..." My father ran over to the radio and turned it off. He began to jump around crazily like a clown, trying to distract our attention from what we had heard. He danced like a dervish in front of the living room mirror. Then he said, "We are going to the beach. Hurry up. Get your things together." Although my parents had decided hours before that the shore would be too crowded on this sunny day. We rushed to get everything together, and drove off to Orchard Beach where we spent the day.

Gradually, over the years, gossip made it known that this young, Jewish man who had been assassinated had gotten fresh with an Italian girl. Like myself, he had been a teacher and a group of female colleagues had somehow been involved in a whispering campaign. And this led to the murder. He had been cleared of some obscure charge, but evidence had been destroyed, and the public knew about it. Anti-semitism was so thick at the time, *you could cut it with a knife.* And somewhere in the background of the anonymous victim had been a beautiful girl. A rape victim. Like April Evesin. But this was more than unclear.

Chapter Fifteen

On my last day in the loony bin, I again enter the little dining room to eat breakfast. Ben the fat man and Jay Elphinston are seated at a table across from one another. There are other places where I could sit, but I am drawn to their table inexorably. All will power has left me. In a trance I shuffle over the linoleum. As I move, the notion enters my mind that this is how all those millions of Jews slaughtered in Auschwitz must have walked to their doom in the gas chambers, even though they knew that death awaited them. I cannot revolt. An immense weight presses all around me and inches my feet toward the very place I should avoid.

I take the vacant chair between them in the center of the tiny table, with a pathetic bowl of porridge that I carefully place in front of me. Porridge. The very food that appears so often in those hideous fairy tales by the Brothers Grimm.

They have been talking and do not interrupt their dialogue for an instant to greet me. Numbly I

The Gangster Papalardo

eat a few spoonfuls of gruel. They are exchanging stories about their days in the armed service. The fat man had been in the army. Elphinston had spent his tour of duty in the navy. Their conversation is animated. Suddenly Elphinston turns to me and asks, "And what branch of the service were you in?"

"I was not in any branch of the armed services," I say. We continue to eat in silence. Then Elphinston again addresses me.

"What is your job?"

"English teacher," I say. "I teach English."

"Then you understand the term 'metaphor'?"

"Yes. A figurative comparison of unlike things not using as or like." I say this with some enthusiasm because the conversation seems to be taking a normal turn. I am almost elated.

"We are going to play a game of metaphors," Elphinston continues.

"Alright," I mumble in puzzlement over his strange statement.

The Gangster Papalardo

Chapter Sixteen

When I got out of the hospital and went back to work, I was so depressed, it was impossible to function in the grand 'professorial' style that was my habit. The chairperson gave me permission to take things easy. So I would start the lesson, give the kids some reading task, which few did, and sit in a dazed state at my desk.

    At home, my wife kept on mumbling phrases like "I want my husband back." For the last month before I left Godspell, stages of my illness expanded. It was a vast emotional tundra I entered. I lost all interest in sex. No word about women passed my lips. I was unable to get erections. Each moment I felt to be my last before a bullet penetrated my brain or I was strangled. Obsessively I wrote and rewrote my will on notebook paper, leaving one part of my stamp collection to my son, another to my daughter. Giving back to the library the numerous books I had stolen over the years, etc. One day in early December, I went to the Granite

The Gangster Papalardo

Bank on Sedgwick Avenue in the Bronx to empty out my safety deposit box. There was nothing of value or importance in the vault, just some old material relating to taxes, so I intended to discard the contents and close the box, saving myself an unnecessary expense. My mother lived around the corner in an old apartment building that had once been a luxury dwelling, and I telephoned her that I would be stopping by.

I entered the bank and gave my request to the guard for access to the vault. He looked up my name in an index file and had a clerk take me down a spiral staircase to the lower floor where the boxes were kept. When I got inside, before I could give anyone the number, I saw a uniformed employee on a ladder manipulating the deposit box I knew was mine, having observed its location on previous visits. It now had some strange knob jutting from the front. Then the man came down and walked over to where I waited.

"What is going on here?" I demanded. "You were doing something to my safety deposit box."

"No. ...No," he said nervously. "The usual maintenance we provide for all the boxes."

I was annoyed, but there was nothing I could do, and it occurred to me that perhaps my suspicions regarding evil intentions were unjust, so I gave him my box number and key.

"I want to close out my rental when I'm through," I said.

The Gangster Papalardo

We went into the interior of the vault and once more he climbed the ladder. When he reached the right level, he twisted off the weird device that jutted from the metal locker. Then he came down and handed over the drawer.

Naturally, I was now very suspicious, so when I went into one of the little rooms provided for privacy, I decided to go through those few papers sequestered for safe keeping.

On the top was a letter concerning various taxes a lawyer had sent and told me to keep. I opened it and immediately saw that instead of a note of several sentences, the page now had three paragraphs and the date had been changed to more than a year closer to the present time. One more item I looked at had been forged or altered I thought, but not with the certainty I felt about the first. I did not bother to go through the other things in the locker, realizing the entire contents was tainted, whether or not other individual items had been transformed, which I probably would not be able to determine accurately.

So *now I would have to throw the whole thing out,* which I had intended doing originally, but without going through the trouble of examining the papers. Why would any of the crap in my vault be of interest to someone else? It made no sense. The documents were of no value even to myself. The tax information was from several years back. Who would do such a thing? And why? Why?

The Gangster Papalardo

I put all the papers in my school attaché case I had carried into the bank for that purpose and closed out the rental service.

When I left the bank, I walked around the corner to where my mother lived. I had the keys to the lobby door and my mother's apartment, so I let myself into the vestibule. Instead of undoing the locks to my mother's place on the ground floor, however, I rang the bell. This was to avoid causing her undue alarm. The neighborhood was deteriorating and anyone might be jiggling the mechanism. Her shuffling gait became discernible as she approached the door. Then I heard her ask who it was as she looked through the peephole.

"It's me Mom," I responded.

Houdini probably spent less time opening the great vault that had been dropped into the Hudson than it took my mother to untwist the various devices that kept her safe from any unwanted guests. Finally, we were face to face.

"Mike am I glad to see you."

We kissed. I removed my coat and put my valise on the dinette table, while she went through the ritual of securing the portal with all the meticulous study of Jack Benny.

"I was just going to make some tea," she said, turning toward me.

"Mom, why don't you move up to Scarsdale where you'd feel safe?"

"O, no. I couldn't do that. I have some old

friends here in the building still. And besides Dr. Goldbloom is still here. He takes care of my nosebleeds. Your father and he were friends you know. Goldbloom is semi-retired, but he still looks after me."

"I know," I said. We had this conversation once a week and the arguments she gave were etched on my mind.

While she fussed with the teapot and cups in the kitchen, I asked her if she remembered the safety deposit key I had given her some time back.

"Yes," she said. "I remember. It's in the breakfront in the sliding drawer. Do you want it?"

I went over to the mahogany breakfront and found the key, which I had told the Granite Bank would be returned to them later in the afternoon. They had warned me when I closed out the rental that I would be billed ten dollars if the duplicate were not given back.

"Mom, did you ever give this key to anyone?"

"What do you mean?" she asked, setting out a dish of cookies.

"Did you ever let anyone have the duplicate key?" I repeated, holding up the article for her inspection.

"No. Why should I have given it to anyone? It's yours."

"Well, Listen Mom. When I went to the bank, some papers in my vault had been forged and others altered, I believe."

"Are you sure?" she asked.

"I'm sure about one of them. I'm not so sure about some others. I mean they're not important. In fact they don't mean anything, and I was going to throw them out anyway. But it does seem strange to say the least."

"Are you certain? It can't be. You must be imagining it."

"I don't think so."

Then she placed her right hand over her chest and sat down. She began to weep and suddenly her nose began to bleed. She put her head back in the same instant she felt the first trickle and pressed to her nose the Kleenex that she always carried in her cleavage.

"I'll get Goldbloom," I said, pushing back my chair.

She signaled for me to sit down again. "No, Don't. It's not serious enough. It'll stop by itself." In a minute or so the bleeding ceased.

Then we had tea together as though nothing had happened, and I let her prattle on about Aunt Lilly and Cousin Helen, as though there had been no mention of the contents of my safety deposit box.

I went into the bathroom before leaving, tore into tiny pieces the shit I had removed from the bank and flushed it all down the tube.

When I left my mother's apartment, I was

not sure whether her nosebleed had been a reaction to my statements or a coincidence. But the few tears she had been unable to suppress immediately before one more of her chronic hemorrhages, hinted that it was an intense response to my words. Tearing did not usually bring on the bleeding from what I knew. These effusions taken together told me she thought I was truly insane or *knew* I was not nuts, but was in some sort of grave danger or felt that I was being driven crazy by a very real predicament she was unable to discuss.

It was two weeks later I learned from an article on page twenty-seven of *The Times* that the president, vice president, chief financial analyst, and manager of the Sedgwick Avenue branch of the Granite Bank, where my papers had been stowed, faced indictments on charges of fraud, embezzlement, and racketeering. They were alleged to be associates of Brooklyn's infamous Carbonni crime family. This information made me wonder if there were any connection between these gangsters and the altered documents I had discovered in my vault. Had Jungian synchronicity led me to appear at the right moment? Sheer coincidence perhaps? Or was there someone who had wanted a reaction from me?

The Gangster Papalardo

Chapter Seventeeen

My teaching gradually improved. I actually got up from my desk occasionally and started to question the students, using the kind of formal lesson plan that it had been my habit to make use of. But I would not sit down with the other teachers to have lunch.

As Christmas approached, a new facet was added to the lunch hour. Music was now being piped over the public address system into the faculty refectory. Some holiday songs and some classical pieces.

A few days before the winter break, I was climbing the stairs from my classroom on the third floor to the teacher's cafeteria. I became aware in my ascent of a passionate Italian opera being played over the loudspeakers. The aria blared as I reached the lunchroom.

I carried my tray of roast beef, salad, and coffee into the nearest of two wings that bracketed either side of *Maxime's,* as one of my ironic colleagues had dubbed our dining facility. This had become my custom of late. No one else was ever there. Solitude is what I sought and escape to some measure from the overwrought opus being inflicted on our patch of contentment. But when I got to my destination, half obscured behind a rounded pillar was Rodney Blackworth – history teacher. Ichabod himself. In the past I had sometimes found myself, out of common courtesy, forced to eat with this fellow, as it was his wont to take a seat next to anyone handy. Now I was especially not pleased to see him. I wanted to be by myself, and Blackworth seldom ceased talking. He seemed almost erotically attached to his own voice. And a fine spittle issued from his mouth every few words, so one was compelled to sit at an angle to his face for this loathsome spray to miss its mark. He was a staunch Catholic to boot. Thus, every response to his chattering had to be gingerly weighed. Furthermore, he was ugly. 'Ugly,' however, barely covers this troll's appearance. Six foot two. Gangly and round shouldered. Orangutan arms. Legs disproportionately long in relation to his torso. Like some fucking cloth marionette. A starved, acne scarred face. Ears that put Dumbo to shame. A nose like the prow of Nelson's flagship – a protuberance by the by that hovered over yellow buckteeth. And very little chin. All this topped by patchy brown hair. Today this gentleman was wearing an outfit I had never seen before. Flung over his spindly

The Gangster Papalardo

shoulders was a navy pea jacket with an insignia on the right arm, the words *Fleet Commander* sewn immediately below the emblem. His attire was completed by a summer white uniform. Some sort of military bar adorned the right side of his blouse.

"I'm teaching The Battle of the Atlantic," Blackworth explained.

"I see," I said. "Very impressive."

"Gets the kids motivated."

"I would guess."

"Sit down."

"Alright," I agreed, not wanting to offend him and being too depressed to hike across to the other rest area some seventy-five yards in an easterly direction. I made certain not to place my chair directly in front of him.

"Ever teach war novels?" he asked.

"Sure. *Red Badge of Courage. Farewell to Arms. All Quiet on the Western Front.*"

"What is your favorite?"

"Depends."

"On what?"

I was only too happy to discuss literature, as it distracted me from graver cares.

"Well, for style, Hemingway's novel is best, although Crane's book is wonderfully written, but the 'moral,' if you can call it that, is foolish, very adolescent. Become a military hero and a 'man,' regardless of the risks. Not realistic. Crane had never been in the military. Hemingway has the right idea. Nothing is worth dying for. Grab your main squeeze and row across Lake Geneva. Remarque's work is best for discouraging any kind of martial spirit. Relentless. The inhuman savagery of war. Remarque had spent four harrowing years on the Western Front."

"So you are against war?"

I had never found Rodney Blackworth so interested in anyone else's ideas. And this should have cautioned me.

"Of course," I replied.

"And the present conflict?"

"Shit. Garbage." I knew the moment these words escaped my lips that it was the wrong response to give this demented ogre. The expression on his face changed and his eyes glittered.

"Why? Don't you think the United States must defend itself?"

"Yes. But I don't think the United States is defending itself in this situation."

"Don't you think we are combating communism."

"No. I don't think so."

"What are your values?"

"Bill of Rights. American ideals."

"Don't you value great art? Michelangelo? Leonardo? The wonderful cathedrals of Europe? Magnificent opera?" At this juncture, Blackworth lifted his arm to indicate the baritone sounds wafting through the air above our heads.

The Gangster Papalardo

"I prefer science, reason, and *Wealth of Nations.*"

"Are you innocent?" Blackworth abruptly inquired. It was the same question Old Man Mountain had asked me in the asylum. I was stumped for a reply.

"Well," I laughed. "Relatively. We're all only relatively ..."

Before I could complete my sentence, Blackworth was on his feet, hovering over me.

"Then prepare to meet your Maker," he shrieked at the top of his lungs. "Your death is imminent. Everytime you see this uniform," he screamed, leaning over me and pushing the open navy pea jacket in my face, "may be your last torment here on earth. So fight the glorious battle. It will be your last." Then he marched out.

At the first explosion of violent words from this psychotic's mouth, I began to tremble. Had this been the first assault on my mind by an initiate of The Eye's goose-stepping flock, I would have risen from my seat and smashed the repulsive freak in his nose. But I had been worn down by the band of harpies who had orchestrated the whole staff against me at the beginning of the term, the terrifying attack at Godspell, that whole thing with lawyer Harbinger, the looting of my safety deposit box, the suffering endured by my family, the total invasion of my privacy, the quiet hostility smoldering around me on my return, the sexual dysfunction and general despair that enveloped my every move. Instead of action, I was paralyzed in brain and body. My head snapped free of my straining neck and rose slowly toward the ceiling of the room, where it floated like some child's castaway balloon in garish disregard of parental anguish. Tears surged from my eyes, as involuntary in their passage as blood lunging from a suddenly inflicted wound. I could no more have halted the shaking of my torso or the spasms in my limbs than I could have stopped the coils of some tremendous snake from enfolding my flesh and bones. This process went on for many minutes.

Chapter Eighteen

The next morning when I got to class for my first lesson of the day, every pupil in the room – even the girls – were wearing some form of navy garb. I began to sweat and felt both nauseous and unsteady. Instead of teaching Browning's *My Last Duchess,* as I intended, I wrote a list of questions on the board and asked the students to answer these at their desks. Then I sat down in a daze.

Every one of my classes was packed with kids impersonating naval personnel of one rank or another. I was reminded of the goddamn bastards who climbed on top of tables in the lunchroom and danced when poor, brave Scoppetti was almost beaten to death for trying to stop the drug trafficking in Doolittle. The whole school had been turned against me. By the end of the day I felt such torment that I could hardly breathe. As I rode home in my battered wreck, every ad on the radio appeared to have at least a few words aimed at intensifying my despair. This is not difficult to do. Someone in power asks for cooperation of a minor sort. The offending phrase is integrated into the advertisement, which costs nothing, and the message is delivered to the audience without diminishing its intended effect. Only the selected target realizes his privacy has been invaded.

When I got home, I wept into a pillow, as I was sure the massive attempt to drive me crazy would end in my murder. Ads now appeared on *television* which contained a few allusions related to my situation. This kind of harassment was intensified and extended over a long period. All the kids and even some of the teachers cooperated with my tormentors. In a school best described as the ninth circle of hell, where the most serious and grotesque crimes were being committed openly on a daily basis and on a scale even Ripley would not believe, *Tresojos* had taken to torturing Woody Allen. It's all talk unless the Mafia gets involved. Then it becomes as palpable as death itself.

It was not only within the confines of Doolittle High School that this pernicious crap took place. Everywhere I went in the city, citizens seemed eager to take part in bothering me. I could not sit down at a lunch counter without people speaking briskly about U-boats or the Bismarck or Admiral Halsey or Commander Doenitz or ensigns and petty officers *ad nauseam*. Everywhere there were whispers of bloody murder, with citizens glancing at their watches to determine precisely how much time I had left. My imagination ran wild trying to pinpoint exactly why these sons-of-bitches wanted to humiliate a thirty-two-year-old English

The Gangster Papalardo

teacher with a wife and two kids. Were they intimating I ought to join the armed forces and fight in Vietnam? And for what? For getting fresh with an Italian girl? And if I did not submit to this perverse punishment, they would make an example of me. Was that it?

Somewhere into the first twelve weeks of this misery, an ad appeared on television for the Emerald Oil Company. Emerald is the largest independent oil company on earth. As everyone knows, it is headed by a fabulous eccentric, Carlson Renfrew Emerald, who happens to be the richest man alive. *Emerald is on your side* quickly became the tag line for each installment of the company's promotion campaign and even featured an actor who looked something like me driving along a highway. Miraculously, my harassment abated and then ceased altogether. I can almost begin to lead a normal life.

But sometime in May, I was greeted by a headline in *The New York Times* that reported Emerald's grandson as having been kidnapped in Sorrento, Italy by a band of communist *provocateurs* calling itself *Red Harvest*. To show the old man they meant business, the boy's right ear was posted to him wrapped in a scarlet bandanna. Ostensibly, *Red Harvest* was demanding a ransom of one-hundred-million dollars. In fact, I believed their demands had something to do with me. After negotiations of about two weeks, the lad was released without further harm. Several days later, the mother-fuckers began to harass me again. Emerald Oil changed its advertising slogan from *Emerald is on your side* to *Make your engine sparkle with Emerald's.* Carlson Renfrew Emerald had been made to see the light. I really was an unsavory, duplicitous coward who deserved to be picked on without mercy, utterly squelched, and perhaps even killed.

I inferred from this episode that the KGB and organized crime were in cahoots, something I had suspected vaguely in a general sense for several years. Maybe they wanted me dead because I had successfully psychoanalyzed myself or because I was one of those rare neurotics who actually read all nine-hundred pages of Smith's *Wealth of Nations.*

Just around the time Emerald changed his tune, *The Times* printed a news article on its front page about an obscure organization called the Department of American Strategic Studies, D.A.S.S. The report centered on how this little known arm of government had been inducing people to commit all kinds of crimes, which its guiding spirit then gave the appearance of solving with amazing dexterity. There were even hints that D.A.S.S. may have had a hand in persuading Oswald to murder Kennedy, using the kind of techniques discussed in *The Hidden Persuaders* and demonstrated in Shakespeare's *Macbeth.* This was

The Gangster Papalardo

in line with my present reasoning about the assassination. Each day another front page account appeared to this effect, slightly different from the previous one. The reports were all written by two famous Pulitzer Prize winning journalists, working alternately. And with each installment, their language crept closer and closer to the words I customarily used in teaching The Bard's Scottish tragedy, until these masterful newsmen were actually using my exact diction, phrasing, and syntax. Naturally, I dared not mention this to anyone since allegations of plagiarism against such venerable figures would only convince people that I was suffering from delusions of grandeur and *confirm* the idea that I was a lunatic whose explanations *should* be discounted. I wondered if D.A.S.S. were not the real name of *Tresojos*. At the same time, of course, these two writers may have been warning those in power to leave me alone because they knew I was right about certain *very important things*.

In August, the executive director of D.A.S.S. who had built his distinguished reputation on fraud, as *The Times* indicated, had a fatal collision with a truck on I 95. An autopsy report stated that just before the accident, the seventy-three-year-old man apparently suffered a massive coronary, which would have killed him anyway, even if he had not swerved into the Emerald Oil tanker coming toward him on the opposite side of the highway. The tanker

The Gangster Papalardo

had emptied its last drops of precious fluid at a Maryland station only minutes before. The trucker was not hurt, and the director was buried with honors in Arlington National Cemetery. Had the articles in *The Times* induced cardiac arrest? Had a heart attack actually occurred? Perhaps, the oil tanker's presence was just happenstance. Maybe the coronary was a result of the crash.

The columns about D.A.S.S. continued for another six weeks on the front page, possibly to distract suspicion from the idea their contents may have had something to do with the executive's death, and they ceased around the time I stopped reading newspapers altogether. But my harassment did not end.

I end up back in the hospital. It is ever the same. Even the man in the yellow bathrobe is still in this shit hole. In fact I can see him now in profile across the enormous room, pivoting toward me, squinting his little pig eyes in my direction. He faces me and shifts his slender torso slightly. His chin rises and points itself in my direction like the beak of some terrible avis that feeds on dead souls. He shuffles toward me, a psychotic nightmare come to life. Indeed, so hypnotic is this image that I cannot for a moment look away. Why? Why does he hold my attention so? And then I realize. I know who he is, though I have never met the man. It is the gangster Papalardo.